DEMIAN

DEMIAN

THE STORY OF
EMIL SINCLAIR'S YOUTH

by Hermann Hesse
translated by Thomas Wayne

Algora Publishing
New York

Library of Congress Cataloging-in-Publication Data —

Hesse, Hermann, 1877–1962.
Names: Hesse, Hermann, 1877–1962, author. | Wayne, Thomas, translator.
Title: Demian : the story of Emil Sinclair's youth / by Hermann Hesse ;
    translated by Thomas Wayne.
Other titles: Demian. English
Description: New York : Algora Publishing, [2022] | Summary: "Hermann
    Hesse's finest novel, Demian is a poetical, lyrical, Jungian journey to
    self-discovery in a fresh and faithful new translation. Set on the verge
    of the First World War, a time like ours when one could smell that "the
    collapse of an old world is getting closer," Demian is a cure for
    nihilism, Face-book, and self-despair"— Provided by publisher.
Identifiers: LCCN 2022016524 (print) | LCCN 2022016525 (ebook) | ISBN
    9781628944822 (trade paperback) | ISBN 9781628944839 (hardcover) | ISBN
    9781628944846 (pdf)
Subjects: LCGFT: Bildungsromans. | Novels.
Classification: LCC PT2617.E85 D413 2022 (print) | LCC PT2617.E85 (ebook)
    | DDC 833/.912—dc23/eng/20220408
LC record available at https://lccn.loc.gov/2022016524
LC ebook record available at https://lccn.loc.gov/2022016525

Printed in the United States

I wanted nothing other than to try to live that which wanted to come out of me on its own. Why was that so very hard?

TABLE OF CONTENTS

Hesse — In Moderation

Hermann Hesse is one of the finest European novelists of the 20th century and Demian is perhaps his finest novel, the novel in which he most succinctly and successfully expressed his favorite theme — the journey to the self.

In *Demian* Hesse tells the story of a young man named Emil Sinclair who finds the meaning of his life through certain signs and symbols, certain mentors and tormentors, certain idols and ideals. These include the enigmatic Max Demian, the flawed musician and antiquarian Pistorius, Jung's archetypes, Nietzsche's Zarathustra, Goethe's Faust, Dostoevsky's Underground Man, Schopenhauer's pessimism.

The bourgeois, the world of light, the moderate and mediocre, the safe path... or the other, darker, more questioning and questionable realm — which will our Emil Sinclair choose? Which will our present world choose? All we know is that something dreadful is about to happen, something earth-shattering, something which will force his hand and ours. Foreboding dreams, presentiments present themselves.

Here Hesse is truly in his element. As Demian says near the end of the novel: "Nobody dreams what doesn't concern him. But it doesn't concern me alone, there you are right... That our world is downright rotten we know. Sinclair, we will live to see this, of which we have often spoken! The world wants to renew itself. It smells of death." And later Demian says: "Perhaps it will be a large war, a very large war. But that too is merely the beginning. The new begins, and the new, for those who cling to the old, will be terrifying. What will you do?"

This novel, then, is not just about Europe on the brink of war in 1914 with the Spanish Flu to follow in 1918; it is not only for that post-war generation. It is also a story for our time, as we look backward to what was and forward to the new, on that fateful journey to self which Hesse presents to us so artfully.

Thomas Wayne

DEMIAN

In order to tell my story, I must begin way back. I would have to, were it possible for me, go back even much farther, to the very first years of my childhood and even beyond them to the distant time of my origin. Poets, when they write novels, are wont to act as if they were God and think they can totally survey and comprehend some person's history and represent it in such a way, as if God Himself might tell it, without any veils, all the essentials. That I cannot do, as little as the poets can do it. My story, however, is more important to me than any poet's is to him; for it is my own, and it is the story of a man — not an invented, a possible, an ideal or otherwise not pre-existing one, but an actual one-time, living man. What that is, an actual living man, that is known today less than ever to be sure, and these men also, of whom each is an expensive, one-time attempt of Nature, are shot to death. Were we not something more than one-time men, could each one of us actually be totally removed from the world with a musket-ball, then it would make sense no more to tell stories. Each man, however, is not only himself, he is also the one-time, quite special, in each case important and remarkable point, where the phenomena of the world intersect, only once in this way and never again. Therefore each man's story is important, eternal, godlike, therefore each man, as long as he lives somehow and fulfills the will of Nature, is wonderful and worthy of every consideration. In each the spirit has assumed form, in each the creature suffers, in each a savior is crucified.

Few know today what man is. Many feel it and die more easily therefore, as I will die more easily when I have finished this story.

A knowing one I dare not call myself. I was a seeker and am one still, but I seek no more in the stars and in books, I begin to listen to the teachings which my blood rustles in me. My story is not pleasant, it is not sweet and harmonious like the invented stories, it smacks of nonsense and confusion, of madness and dream, like the lives of all men who want to deceive themselves no longer with lies.

The life of each man is a way to himself, the attempt at a way, the pointing out of a path. No man has ever been utterly and completely himself; yet each strives to become it, one dull, one brighter, each as he can. Each carries remnants from his birth, slime and eggshells of a primeval world, with him until the end. Many never become man, remain frog, remain lizard, remain ant. Many are man above and fish below. But each is a cast of Nature towards man. The origins are common to us all, the mothers, we all come from the same gullet; but each strives, an attempt and cast from the depths, to attain his own goal. We can understand each other; but to interpret each can only do for himself.

Chapter One. Two Worlds

I begin my story with an experience of the time when I was ten years old and attended the Latin school of our small town.

Much wafts towards me there and stirs me on the inside with woe and with cheerful shudders, dark alleys and bright houses and towers, clock-strikings and human faces, rooms full of commodiousness and warm comfort, rooms full of mystery and deep ghost-fear. It smells of warm confinement, of rabbit and serving maids, of household remedies and dried fruit. Two worlds ran through one another there, from two poles day and night came there.

The one world was the paternal roof, but it was even narrower yet, it actually embraced only my parents. This world was well-known to me for the most part; it meant mother and father, it meant love and strictness, model and school. To this world belonged mild gleam, clarity, and cleanliness, here soft friendly speech, washed hands, clean clothes, and good manners were at home. Here the morning hymn was sung, here Christmas was celebrated. In this world there were straight lines and roads that led to the future, there was duty and debt, bad conscience and confession, forgiveness and good intentions, love and reverence, Bible verse and wisdom. To this world one had to attach oneself, so that life would be clear and pure, handsome and ordered.

The other world, meanwhile, already began amidst our own house and was completely different, smelled different, spoke different, promised and demanded something different. In this second world there were serving maids and travelling artisans, ghost stories and whiffs of scandal, there was a colorful flood of monstrous, alluringly terrible, puzzling things, matters like slaughterhouse and prison, drunkards and fishwives, calving cows, broken-down horses, stories of break-ins, murders, suicides. All these beautiful and dreadful, wild and cruel things there were all around, in the next alley, in the next house; policemen and tramps ran around, drunkards beat their wives, throngs of young girls issued nightly from factories, old women could employ magic and make one sick, robbers lived in the woods, arsonists were captured by local law authorities — everywhere this second, violent world issued and exhaled its scent, everywhere, only not in our rooms, where mother and father were. And that was very good. It was wonderful that here by us there was peace, order and quiet, duty and good conscience, forgiveness and love — and wonderful that there was all the other thing too, all that loud and garish, gloomy and powerful stuff from which one could still escape with a leap to one's mother.

And what was strangest was how the two worlds bordered each other, how close together they were! For example, our maidservant Lina, when in the evening at devotion she sat in the living room by the door and with her clear voice sang along with us, her washed hands laid on the smoothly-spread apron, then she belonged completely to father and mother, to us, in lightness and rightness. Immediately thereafter in the kitchen or in the woodshed, when she told me the story of the little man without a head, or when by the butcher in his small shop she argued with the neighborhood women, then she was a different person, belonged to a different world, was encompassed in mystery. And so it was with everything, most of all with me myself. Certainly, I belonged to the light and righteous world, I was my parents' child; but wherever I directed my eye and ear, everywhere the other was there, and I lived in the other too, although it was unfamiliar and sinister to me, although one regularly had a bad conscience and anxiety there. At times I even dwelt with the greatest delight in the forbidden world, and often the return into the light — as necessary and good as it might be — was almost like a return into the less beautiful, into the more boring and more tedious. Sometimes I knew: my goal in life was to become just like my parents, so light and pure, so superior and orderly; but to get there the way was long; to get there one had to sit at school and study and pass trials and tests, and the way always led to and past the other, darker world, through and throughout it, and it was not at all impossible that one might stay there and be swallowed up in it. There were stories of lost sons, to whom it had thus gone; I had read them with passion. There the return home to the father and to the good was so redeeming and magnificent, I thoroughly felt that this alone was the right, good, and desirable thing, and yet the part of the story that played out among the evil and lost ones was the more alluring by far, and were one allowed to say and admit it, it was actually at times a real pity that the prodigal one did penance and was found again. But a person didn't say this and didn't think it either. It was only somehow existent, as a presentiment and a possibility, way down in one's feeling. When I pictured the devil to myself, I could very well think of him down below on the street, disguised or open, or at the annual fair, or in a tavern, but never by us at home.

My sisters as well belonged to the light world. They were, so they often seemed to me, in their essence much nearer to my father and mother; they were better, more mannered, more error-free than me. They had flaws, they had bad habits, but it seemed to me, not going very deep, which was not true of me, where the contact with evil became often so heavy and tormenting, where the dark world stood so much nearer. Sisters were, like parents, to be treated with consideration and esteem, and if you had quarreled with them, afterward before your own conscience you were always the bad one, the instigator, the one who had to ask for forgiveness. For in offending the sisters you offended the parents, the good and the commanding ones. There were secrets which I could share with the most reprehensible street-Arab far sooner than with my sisters. On good days, when it was light and my conscience was in order, then it was often priceless to play with my sisters, to be good and well-behaved with them and to see myself in a gallant and noble aspect. So it must be, were one an angel! That was the highest state we knew, and we thought it sweet and wonderful to be angels, encompassed by a light sound and aroma like Christmas and happiness. Oh how seldom such days and hours occurred! Often while at play, at some good, harmless, allowed playing, I got into such a passion and rage it became too much for my sisters, which led to conflict and unhappiness, and when this wrath came over me then I was horrible and did and said things, of whose reprehensibility, even while I did and said them, I felt deeply and ardently. Then came harsh, gloomy hours of regret and remorse, and then the painful moment when I asked for forgiveness, and then again a ray of light, a quiet, thankful happiness without discord, for hours or moments.

I went to the Latin school; the burgomaster's son and the head forester's son were in my class and came to me at times, wild lads and yet belongers to the good, licensed world. In spite of that I had close relations with neighborhood boys, public school students, whom we otherwise despised. With one of them must I begin my story.

On a free afternoon — I was little more than ten years old — I was going around with two boys from the neighborhood. Then a bigger one came up, a strong and raw youth of about thirteen years, a public school student, the son of a tailor. His father was a drinker and the whole family had a bad reputation. I was well acquainted with Franz Kromer, I was afraid of him, and it did not please me when he joined us now. He already had manly mannerisms and imitated the stride and speech habits of the young factory hands. Under his leadership we climbed down next to the bridge on the riverbank and hid ourselves from the world under the first arch of the bridge. The narrow edge between the vaulted brick wall and the languid flowing water consisted of nothing but refuse, fragments and rubbish, tangled bundles of rusted iron wire and other sweepings. At times one could find useful things there; under Franz Kromer's leadership we had to search the area and show him what we found. Then he either pocketed it or threw it out in the water. He told us to be on the lookout for objects made of lead, brass, or tin; these he pocketed all to himself, even an old comb made of horn. In his company I felt myself very oppressed, not because I knew my father would have forbidden me this society had he known about it, but out of fear of Franz himself. I was glad that he received me and treated me like the others. He commanded and we obeyed; it was like an old custom, although it was my first time together with him.

Finally we sat down on the ground; Franz spat into the water and looked like a man; he spat through a gap in his teeth and hit whatever he wanted. A conversation began, and the boys started singing their praises and boasting with all sorts of schoolboy heroics and evil pranks. I kept silent and yet feared that it was precisely in my being silent that the wrath of Kromer would manage to fall upon me. My two comrades had distanced themselves from me from the beginning and made themselves acquainted with him; I was a stranger among them and felt that my attire and manner were challenging to them. As a Latin school student and gentleman's little son, Franz couldn't possibly be fond of me, and the two others, this I felt for sure, would, as soon as it came to it, disown me and leave me in the lurch.

At last out of sheer anxiety I began to tell a story too. I made up a big robbery tale, of which I was the hero. In a garden by the corner mill, I said, I along with a comrade had at night stolen a whole sack full of apples, and not some ordinary ones, nothing but Reinetten and Goldparmänen, the best sort. Out of the dangers of the moment I took refuge in this story, the invention and narration of which came naturally to me. In order not to cease at once again and perhaps become entangled in something worse, I let my entire art shine. One of us, I said, stood on guard the whole time while the other was in the tree and threw the apples down, and the sack got so heavy that at last we had to open it again and leave behind half, but we came back a half an hour later and took them as well.

When I was done, I hoped for some applause; at last I had warmed up and was intoxicated by my fable telling. The two smaller ones were silent, waiting; Franz Kromer, however, looked at me piercingly with half-pinched eyes and asked in a threatening voice: "Is that true?"

"Yes indeed," I said.

"Really and truly so?"

"Yes, really and truly," I protested defiantly while inwardly I suffocated with fear.

"Can you swear to it?"

I was very scared, but I said yes at once.

"Then say: By God and eternal bliss!"

I said: "By God and eternal bliss."

"All right," he said and turned away.

With that I thought everything was fine and was happy when he arose quickly and took the way back. When we were on the bridge, I timidly said I had to head home now.

"That is not so pressing," laughed Franz, "we're going the same way after all."

Slowly he sauntered along, and I dared not run off; he, however, actually took the way to our house. When we were there, when I saw our front door and the big brass knocker, the sun in the windows and the curtains in my mother's room, then I drew a deep breath of relief. O return home! O good blessed return home, into the light, into peace!

As I quickly opened the door and slipped in, there, behind me, ready to pounce, Franz Kromer crowded his way in along with me. In the cool, gloomy tiled passageway, which only received its light here from the courtyard, he stood by me, held me by the arm and softly said: "No so fast, you!"

Terrified, I looked at him. His grip on my arm was firm like iron. I pondered over what he might have in mind and whether he intended to do me wrong. If I were to scream now, I thought, scream loud and violently, would someone from above be here quickly enough perhaps to save me? But I gave it up.

"What is it?" I asked. "What do you want?"

"Not much. I simply have to ask you something else. The others don't need to hear it."

"Is that so? Indeed, what more do I have to say to you? I have to go up, you know."

"You do know," said Franz Kromer softly, "to whom the orchard by the corner mill belongs?"

"No, I don't know. The miller, I believe."

Franz had slung his arm around me and drew me now quite close to him so that I had to see his face right next to mine. His eyes were evil, he smiled wickedly, and his face was full of ferocity and power.

"Yes, my young man, I can certainly tell you to whom the garden belongs. I've known for quite some time that the apples were stolen and I also know that the man said he would give anyone two marks who could tell him who had stolen the fruit."

"Dear God!" I cried. "But you wouldn't tell him a thing, would you?"

I felt it would be useless to appeal to his sense of honor. He was from the other world, for him betrayal was no crime. I felt this exactly. In these matters the people from the "other" world were not like us.

"Tell nothing?" laughed Kromer. "Dear friend, do you mean then I should become a counterfeiter in order to make myself a couple of marks? I'm a poor fellow, I don't have a rich father like you, and so to make two marks I have to earn them. Perhaps he'll pay even more.'"

Suddenly he let me go again. Our entrance hallway no longer smelt of peace and security, the world collapsed around me. He would denounce me, I was a criminal, my father would be informed, perhaps the police would even come. All the terror of chaos threatened me, all things ugly and dangerous had been summoned against me. That I had not stolen a thing was of no importance at all. Besides, I had sworn. My God, my God!

Tears welled up in me. I felt I had to buy myself off and grasped despairingly into all my pockets. No apple, no pocket knife, nothing at all was there. Then I thought of my watch. It was an old silver watch and it didn't run, I carried it "just because." It came from our grandmother. Quickly I pulled it out.

"Kromer," I said, "listen, you must not give me up, that would not be nice of you: I'll present you with my watch, look here; unfortunately, I have nothing else at all. You can have it, it's made of silver, and the workmanship is good, it has only one little flaw, it needs to be repaired."

He smiled and took the watch in his large hand. I looked at this hand and felt how raw and deeply hostile to me it was, how it grasped at my life and peace.

"It's made of silver —" I said shyly.

"I couldn't care less about your silver and your old watch there!" he said with profound contempt. "First go repair it yourself!"

"But Franz," I cried trembling with fear lest he might run away. "Wait a moment, would you! Take the watch at least! It's really made of silver, really and truly. And I simply have nothing else."

He looked at me cool and contemptuously.

"Well, you know to whom I'm going. Or I can tell the police also, I know the constable well."

He turned to go. I held him back by the sleeve. It could not be allowed. I would much rather have died than to suffer all that was to come if he went away thus.

"Franz," I implored, hoarse with excitement, "don't do anything foolish! It's just a joke, right?"

"Yes indeed, a joke, but for you it could become expensive."

"Tell me truly, Franz, what I should do! I'll do anything at all!"

He surveyed me with his pinched-in eyes and laughed again.

"Don't be so stupid!" he said with false good-naturedness. "You know just as well as I — I can earn two marks, and I am not a rich man that can throw them away, this you know. You are rich, however, you even have a watch. You need only give me the two marks, then everything will be fine."

I grasped the logic. But two marks! For me that was as much and as unattainable as ten, as a hundred, as a thousand marks. I had no money. There was a little savings box that my mother kept for me; from uncle visits and such occasions there were a few ten- and five-pfennig pieces within. Otherwise I had nothing. I still received no allowance at the time.

"I have nothing," I said sadly. "I have no money at all. But I'll give you everything else. I have a cowboy and Indian book, and soldiers, and a compass. I'll fetch them for you."

Kromer merely jerked with his bold, wicked mouth and spat on the floor.

"Stop the chatter!" he said commandingly. "You can keep your ragtag trash. A compass! Don't even make me angry now, you hear, and hand over the money!"

"I have none, I never get any money. I can't do anything about it!"

"All right then you bring me the two marks tomorrow. I'll wait for you after school down by the marketplace. With that we're done. If you don't bring any money, then you'll see for sure!"

"Yes, but where shall I get it then? Dear God, if I just don't have any —"

"There's money enough at your house. That's your affair. So tomorrow after school. And I'm telling you: if you don't bring it —" He shot me a frightful glance, spat once more and vanished like a shadow.

I could not go upstairs. My life was destroyed. I thought about running away and never returning, or drowning myself. But I had no clear image. I sat down in the dark on the lowest step of our staircase, crept narrowly within myself and resigned myself to the calamity. Lena found me there weeping when she came down with a basket to fetch wood.

I entreated her to say nothing about it upstairs, and went on up. On a rack near the glass door hung my father's hat and my mother's parasol. Home and tenderness streamed towards me from all these things; my heart greeted them beseechingly and thankfully, as the Prodigal Son to the sight and smell of the old native chambers. But all that no longer belonged to me now, that all was bright father- and mother-world, and I was sunk deeply and full of guilt in the foreign flood, ensnared in adventure and sin, threatened by a foe and expecting perils, anguish, and shame. The hat and parasol, the good old sandstone floor, the large picture over the entrance hall wardrobe and coming from within the living room out here the voice of my elder sister, all this was dearer, more tender and precious than ever, but it was no longer a comfort and a sure blessing, it was nothing but a reproach. All this was no longer mine, I could not take part in its serenity and quiet. I carried mud on my feet that I could not wipe off on the mat, I brought shadow along with me of which this home-world knew nothing. How many secrets I already possessed, how much anxiety, but it was all fun and games compared to that which I had brought with me into these rooms today. Fate ran after me, hands were stretched out toward me, before which even any mother could not protect me, about which she was not permitted to know. Whether now my crime was a theft or a lie (had I not sworn a false oath by God and eternal bliss?) — that was all one. My sin was not this or that, my sin was that I had shaken hands with the devil. Why had I gone along with it? Why had I obeyed Kromer, more so than my own father? Why had I made up that story about the theft? Given myself criminal airs as though they were heroic deeds? Now the devil held my hand, now the enemy was here behind me.

For a moment I no longer felt afraid for the morrow but above all for the terrible certainty that my way from now on would lead downhill and into darkness. I sensed distinctly that from my transgression new transgressions must follow, that my presence among my sisters, my greeting and kissing my parents was a lie, that I carried a fate and a secret with me that I had to hide inside.

A moment of confidence and hope flashed up in me when I view my father's hat. I would tell him everything, would accept his judgment and his punishment and make him my confidant and savior. It would only be a penance, as I had often had to endure, a grave bitter hour, a grave and rueful bid for forgiveness.

How sweet that sounded! How handsomely that enticed! But there was nothing to it. I knew that I now had a secret, a debt that I alone had to pay the penalty for. Perhaps I was just now at the parting of the ways, perhaps from this hour on I would belong to the bad forever, share secrets with the wicked, depend on them, obey them, become like them. I had acted the man and hero, now I had to bear what followed hence.

I was glad that my father detained me about my wet shoes when I entered. It distracted him, he didn't notice the worse thing, and I was allowed to endure a reproach that I could secretly transfer over to the other. With that a strange new feeling glistened in me, an evil and cutting feeling full of barbs: I felt superior to my father! I felt, for a moment, a certain contempt for his ignorance, his scolding over the wet boots seemed trivial to me. "If only you knew!" I thought and it struck me like a criminal being tried for stealing a roll while he should have been on trial for murder. It was an ugly and untoward feeling, but it was strong and had a deep attraction, and it enchained me more firmly than any other thought to my secret and my guilt. Perhaps, I thought, Kromer has gone to the police by now and has turned me in, and thunderstorms are gathering themselves over my head, while here I am being viewed as a little child!

From this whole experience, so far as it has been related hitherto, this moment was the most important and lasting one. It was the first tear in the sanctity of the father, it was the first cut in the pillar upon which my childhood rested, and which every man before he can become himself, must destroy. Out of these experiences, which no one sees, consists the inner, essential line of our own destiny. Such a cut and tear grows back together, it gets healed up and is forgotten, but in the most secret chamber it lives and bleeds further.

I immediately felt dread at this new feeling, I would have liked to kiss my father's feet at once thereupon, in order to apologize to him. But one cannot apologize for something essential, and this a child feels and knows as well and as deeply as any wise man.

I felt the necessity to reflect on my situation, to speculate on ways for the morrow; but I didn't get to it. I spent the whole evening simply getting accustomed to the changed atmosphere in our living room. Wall clock and table, Bible and mirror, bookcase and pictures on the wall were as it were taking their departure from me; with a freezing heart I had to look on as my world, as my good, fortunate life became a thing of the past and detached itself from me, and had to sense how with new, absorbing roots outside in the dark and alien world I was being anchored and held fast. For the first time I tasted death, and death tasted bitter, for it is birth, anxiety, and dread of a terrible innovation.

I was glad when I finally lay in my bed! Previously as a last purgatory there was evening prayers, and we had thereto sung a hymn that was one of my favorites. Alas, I did not sing along, and each note was gall and poison to me. I did not pray along when my father pronounced the blessing, and when he ended: "— be with us all!", then with a spasm I was swept away from this circle. The grace of God was with them all, but no longer with me. Cold and deeply weary I walked away.

In bed, after I lay there awhile, as warmth and security enclosed me lovingly, my heart wandered back once more into anxiety, fluttered uneasily concerning the past. My mother had as always wished me good night, her step still resounded in the room, the light of her candle still glowed in the chink of the door. Now, I thought, now she will come back once more, she has sensed something, she will give me a kiss and ask, ask kindly and full of promise, and then I can cry, then the lump in my throat will melt, then I will embrace her and tell her about it, then all will be well, then salvation will be at hand! And even after the chink in the door had grown dark, I still listened awhile and was of the opinion it had to and had to be.

Then I returned to my things and looked my enemy in the eye. I saw him clearly, his one eye he had pinched in, his mouth laughed roughly, and as I looked at him and the inescapable ate into me, he became bigger and uglier, and his evil eye flashed devilishly. He was close by me until I fell asleep, then, however, I didn't dream of him nor of today, but I dreamed we were riding in a boat, my parents and my sisters and I, and we were surrounded by nothing but the peace and splendor of a vacation day. I awoke in the middle of the night, still felt the aftertaste of this bliss, still saw the white summer clothes of my sisters shimmering in the sun and fell out of all this paradise back into that which was, and stood once again opposite the enemy with the evil eye.

In the morning, when my mother came in hurriedly and cried that it was already late and why was I still in bed, I looked ill, and when she asked me if something was wrong, I vomited.

Something seemed to be gained by this. I dearly loved being a little sick and being allowed to remain lying in bed all morning long with chamomile tea, listening how my mother tidied up in the next room, and how Lina received the butcher outside in the entrance-hall. Morning without school was something magical and fabulous — was not the same sun against which in the school the green curtains were let down. But that too failed to please today and had a false ring to it.

Ah, if only I were dead! But I was only slightly unwell, as often before, and there was nothing to be done about it. It protected me from school, but it in no way protected me from Kromer, who was waiting for me at eleven o'clock in the marketplace. And my mother's friendliness was this time without comfort; it was burdensome and caused pain. I feigned soon falling asleep again and mused. It didn't help at all, I had to be in the marketplace at eleven. Therefore I got up at ten o'clock quietly and said that I was well once more. That meant, as usual in such cases, that I either had to go back to bed or go to school in the afternoon. I had formed a plan.

Without money I dare not come to Kromer. I had to get hold of the little savings box that belonged to me. There was not enough money inside, that I knew, not nearly enough; but it was still something, and my suspicion told me that something was better than nothing and Kromer would at least be appeased.

I felt bad when in my stocking feet I snuck into my mother's room and took my box out of her writing desk; but it was not as bad as yesterday's affair. The beating of my heart choked me, and it didn't get better when beneath the staircase upon first examination I found that the box was locked. To break it apart would be easy, there was only a thin tin grating to tear asunder; but the tearing hurt, for only with this had I committed theft. Until then I had only nibbled on the sly, sweets and fruit. This now was stolen, although it was my own money. I sensed how I once more was a step closer to Kromer and his world, how bit by bit things went downhill so nicely and did it out of spite anyway. I counted the money nervously, in the box it had sounded so full, now in the hand it was miserably little. It was sixty-five pfennigs. I hid the box on the ground floor, held the money in my closed hand and walked out of the house, different than I ever was before when I went through the door. Upstairs somebody called after me, so it seemed to me; I went away quickly.

There was still a lot of time; I snuck off along byways through the alleys of a changed town, under never-seen clouds, past houses that looked at me and people that viewed me with suspicion. On the way it occurred to me that a school comrade of mine had once found a thaler at the cattle market. Gladly would I have prayed that God might perform a miracle and let me make such a find. But I no longer had a right to pray. And even then the box would not be whole again.

Franz Kromer saw me from afar, yet he came slowly up to me and seemed not to notice me. When he was close, he gave me a commanding wink, that I should follow him, and went without looking around a single time, quietly further, down the Strohgasse and over the foot-bridge, until he halted by the last houses in front of a new building. No work was going on there, the walls stood bare, without doors and windows. Kromer looked around and went in through the entrance, with me following. He stepped behind the wall, beckoned to me and reached his hand out.

"Do you have it?" he asked coolly.

I drew a clenched hand out of my pocket and emptied my money into his flat hand. He had counted it even before the last fiver had ceased to sound.

"That's sixty-five pfennigs," he said and looked at me.

"Yes," I said shyly. "That's all I have; it's too little, I knew well. But it's all I have. I have no more."

"I took you for being more sensible," he chided me with an almost mild rebuke. "Among honorable men there should be order. I would not take from you what is not right, this you know. Take your nickels back, there! The other — you know who — doesn't try to haggle me down. He pays."

"But I tell you I haven't got any more. It was my entire savings."

"That's your affair. But I don't want to make you unhappy. You still owe me one mark, thirty-five pfennigs. When do I get it?"

"Oh, you'll get it for sure, Kromer! I don't know just when — perhaps I'll have more soon, tomorrow or the day after. You understand, of course, that I can't tell my father."

"That's not my concern. I'm not out to do you any harm. I could have my money before lunch, you see, and I'm poor. You have nice clothes on and you eat better at lunch than I do. But I won't say anything. As far as I'm concerned I can wait a little. Day after tomorrow I'll whistle for you, in the afternoon, then you can set things right. You know my whistle?"

He whistled in front of me, I had often heard him do so.

"Yes," I said, "I know it."

He went away, as though I didn't belong with him, it was a business arrangement between us, nothing further.

Even today, I believe, Kromer's whistle would terrify me, if suddenly I heard it again. From now on I heard it often, it seemed to me, I heard it again and over again. There was no place, no play, no work, no thought where this whistle did not penetrate, this whistle which made me dependent, which now was my fate. Often I was in our little flower garden, which I loved dearly on those soft, colorful autumn afternoons, and an odd impulse bade me to take up boyish games once more from earlier times; I played, so to speak, a boy who was younger than I, who was still good and free, innocent and secure. But in the middle therein, always expected and still always terribly disturbing and surprising, sounded the Kromerish whistle from somewhere, cutting off the thread, destroying the flights of fancy. Then I had to go, had to follow my tormentor to nasty and ugly places, had to render an account and be warned to pay up. The whole thing lasted perhaps a few weeks, but to me, however, it seemed like years, it seemed an eternity. I seldom had any money, a fiver or a groschen, which was stolen from the kitchen table, when Lina left the shopping basket standing there. Each time I was reproached by Kromer and overloaded with contempt; I was the one who was cheating him and wanted to deny him his due right, it was I who was stealing from him, it was I who was making him unhappy! Not often in my life has distress mounted so near to the heart, never have I felt greater hopelessness, greater dependency.

The savings box I had filled with play money and returned to its place, nobody asked about it. But any day this could also come crashing in upon me. Even more than of Kromer's rough whistling I was often afraid of my mother, when she softly stepped toward me — had she not come to ask about the box?

Since I had appeared many times by my devil, he began to torture me and use me in a different way. I had to work for him. He had to run errands for his father, I had to take care of them for him. Or he charged me with completing something difficult, hopping on one leg for ten minutes, pinning a scrap of paper on the skirt of a passerby. Many nights in dreams I would carry on these torments and lie in the sweat of a nightmare.

For a time I became ill. I threw up often and easily caught cold; nights, however, I lay in sweat and heat. My mother felt that something was not right and showed me much sympathy, which tortured me, because I could not confide to her in return.

One time at night, when I was already in bed, she brought me a piece of chocolate. It was a reminder of earlier years, when in the evening, when I had been well-behaved, I would often receive such bits of solace in order to fall asleep. Now she stood there and proffered me the piece of chocolate. It caused me such woe that I could only shake my head. She asked me what was wrong, she stroked my hair. I could only utter: "No! No! I don't want anything." She put the chocolate on the night stand and left. When she wanted to ask me about it at other times I acted as if I knew nothing more concerning it. One time she brought the doctor, who examined me and prescribed cold washings in the morning.

My condition at that time was a kind of madness. Amidst the ordered peace of our house I lived timid and tortured like a ghost, took no part in the lives of the others, rarely forgot myself for an hour. Toward my father, who often irritatedly called me to account, I was closed and cold.

Chapter Two. Cain

The rescue from my torments came from a quite unexpected quarter, and at the same time with it came something new into my life that has affected it to this very day.

A new student had just entered into our Latin school. He was the son of a well-to-do widow who had moved to our town, and he wore mourning-crepe on his sleeve. He was in a higher grade than I and was several years older, but he soon attracted everyone's attention, including mine. This remarkable student seemed to be much older than he looked, on no one did he make the impression of being a boy. Among us childish youths he acted foreign and finished like a man, or rather like a gentleman. He was not popular, he took part in no games, even less in rough-housing, only his self-confident and decisive tone toward the teachers pleased the others. His name was Max Demian.

One day it happened, as it did in our school now and then, that for some reason or another a second class even was placed in our very large classroom. It was Demian's class. We little ones had Bible stories, the bigger ones had to write an essay. While the story of Cain and Abel was being drummed into our heads, I looked over at Demian a lot, whose face particularly fascinated me, and saw this intelligent, light, uncommonly steadfast face bent attentively and ingeniously over his work; he didn't look like a student at all, but like a researcher pursuing his own problems. He was not actually agreeable to me; on the contrary, I had something against him, he seemed too superior and cool, he was all too challengingly secure in his being, and his eyes had the expression of a grown-up — one which children never love — a bit sad with flashes of mockery therein. Yet I couldn't stop looking at him, whether he pleased me or pained me; if he were to hardly glance at me, however, then I withdrew my glance terrified. When I reflect on it today, how he looked as a student at that time, then I can say: he was in every respect different from all others, thoroughly unique and personally stamped, and strikingly so — at the same time, however, he did everything not to be striking, carried and behaved himself like a disguised prince who is among farmboys and makes every effort to appear like one of them.

On the way home from school he walked behind me. When the others had dispersed, he overtook me and greeted me. Even this greeting, although he imitated our schoolboy tone thereby, was so grown-up and polite.

"Shall we go a piece further together?" he kindly asked. I was flattered and nodded. Then I described to him where I lived.

"Ah, there?" he said with a smile. "I know the house all right. Such a remarkable thing is mounted above your doorway, it interested me immediately."

I had no idea at all what he meant and was astounded that he seemed to know our house better than I did. It had probably existed as a keystone over the doorway arch, a coat of arms of sorts, but with the passing of time it was worn flat and had frequently been painted over; with us and our family it had, so far as I knew, nothing to do.

"I know nothing about it," I said shyly. "It is a bird or some such thing, it must be quite old. The house is said to have belonged to a cloister at some earlier time."

"That could well be," he nodded. "Take a good look at it some time! Such things are often quite interesting. I believe it is a sparrow hawk."

We walked further, I was very ill at ease. All of a sudden Demian laughed, as something struck him as funny.

"Yes, you know I was present there in your class," he said gaily. "The story of Cain, who bore that mark on his forehead, right? Does it please you?"

No, anything that we had to learn was seldom pleasing to me. I didn't dare say it, however, it was as if a grown-up were speaking to me. I said I found the story quite good.

Demian clapped me on the shoulder.

"You don't need to put on an act for me, my dear fellow. But the story is in fact downright remarkable, I believe, it is far more remarkable than most others offered as instruction. The teacher really didn't say much about it, just the usual stuff about God and sin and so forth. But I believe —," he interrupted himself, smiled, and asked: "Does this interest you however?"

"Yes, I believe thus," he went on, "one can also apprehend this story of Cain quite differently. Most things we are taught are indeed quite true and correct, but one can also look at them all differently from the way teachers do and mostly they then make much better sense. With this Cain, for example, and the mark on his forehead one cannot be rightly satisfied at all, such as it is explained to us. Don't you also find it so? That someone kills his brother in a quarrel can certainly happen after all, and that afterwards he takes fright and knuckles under, is also possible. But that for his cowardice he is specially distinguished with an order which protects him and drives fear into all others is indeed downright peculiar."

"To be sure," I said with interest: the subject began to grab me. "But how else should one explain the story?"

He struck me on the shoulder.

"It's quite simple! That which was on hand and with which the story took its beginning was the mark. Here was a man who had something in his face that caused fear in others. They didn't dare touch him, he made a strong impression on them, he and his children. Maybe, or certainly, it was not, however, really a mark on his forehead, such as a postmark, in life these things seldom happen so crudely. Much likelier it was a hardly perceptible uncanny something, a little more spirit and boldness in his look than people were accustomed to. This man had power, one shied away from this man. He had a 'mark.' They could explain this as they wanted. And 'they' always want what is convenient for them and puts them in the right. They feared Cain's children for having a 'mark.' Thus they explained the mark not as that which it was, as a mark of distinction, but as the opposite. They said, the fellows with this mark are uncanny, and this they were too. People with courage and character are always very uncanny to other people. That a race of the fearless and uncanny was running around there was very inconvenient, and so they attached a nick-name and a fable to this race, to take vengeance on it, to make up a little bit for all their outstanding fear. — Do you get it?"

"Yes — that means — Cain then was really not evil at all, was he? And the whole story in the Bible is actually not even true?"

"Yes and no. Such old, age-old stories are always true, but they are not always so recorded and not always so explained as they would rightly be. In short, I mean this Cain was a first-rate fellow, and merely because they were afraid of him they hanged this story on him. The story was simply a rumor, the sort of thing that people chatter about, and it was quite true in so far as Cain and his children really did carry a kind of mark and were different from most other people."

I was greatly astounded.

"And so you believe that stuff about the murder isn't true either?" I asked, deeply moved.

"Oh, of course! Certainly that is true. The strong one slew a weaker one. Whether it was really his brother, that is indeed open to doubt. It is not important, in the end all men are brothers. Thus a stronger man killed a weaker one. Perhaps it was a heroic deed, perhaps not. At any rate, however, the other weak ones were now full of anxiety, they complained bitterly, and when they were asked: 'Why don't you simply kill him also?' then they didn't say 'Because we are cowards,' but instead they said: 'One cannot. He has a mark. God has set a mark upon him!' In some such way the swindle came into being. — Well, I'm holding you up. Adieu then!"

He turned into the Altgasse and left me alone, more astonished than ever before. Hardly was he gone when all that he had said to me appeared quite incredible! Cain a noble man, Abel a coward! The mark of Cain a mark of distinction! It was absurd, it was blasphemous and impious. Where did that leave our dear God? Hadn't he accepted Abel's offering, didn't he love Abel? — No, stuff and nonsense! And I suspected that Demian had amused himself at my expense and wanted to lure me onto slippery ice. A damned clever fellow he was indeed, and he could talk, but like this — no —

Never before had I pondered so much over some Biblical or any other kind of story. And never yet had I so completely forgotten that Franz Kromer for such a long time, hours long, a whole evening long. At home I read the story once more through, as it stood in the Bible; it was short and distinct, and it was quite mad to search there for some special, secret meaning. Then any killer could declare himself as God's darling! No, it was nonsense. Only the manner was nice, the way Demian could say such things, so light and pretty, as if everything were self-evident, and with those eyes besides!

Something certainly was not quite in order with me, it was even in great disorder. I had lived in a light and clean world, I had myself been a kind of Abel, and now I was stuck so deep in the "other," had fallen and sunken so low, and yet at bottom there wasn't very much I could do about it! So what was that all about? Yes, and now a recollection flashed up in me which for a moment almost took my breath away. On that wicked evening, when my present misery began, there was that which took place with my father, there, for a moment, I had as if all at once seen through and despised his light world and wisdom! Yes, there I myself, who was Cain and bore the mark, I imagined that this mark was no shame, it was a mark of distinction, and through my malice and my mishap I stood higher than my father, higher than the good and the pious.

It was not in this form of clear thinking that I experienced the matter at that time, but all this was contained therein, it was only a flaming-up of feelings, of odd stirrings, which did damage and yet filled me with pride.

When I recollected — how strangely Demian had spoken about the fearless and the faint-hearted! How curiously he had explained the mark on Cain's forehead! How his eye, his remarkable grown-up's eye, had oddly gleamed thereby! And it crossed my mind unclearly: — is not he himself, this Demian, not some kind of Cain? Why does he defend him, if he doesn't feel akin to him? Why does he have such power in his glance? Why does he speak so scornfully of the "others," of the fearful ones, which are actually after all the pious and those whom God is well-pleased with?

I came to no end with these thoughts. A stone had fallen into the well, and the well was my young soul. And for a long, very long time this matter with Cain, the murder and the mark was the point from which my attempts at knowledge, doubt and criticism all took their departure.

I noticed that the other students were also much taken up with Demian. Of the story concerning Cain I had told nobody anything, but he seemed to interest others as well. At least there were many rumors in circulation about the "newbie." If only I still knew them all, each would shed a light on him, each would provide an explanation. I only know it was first divulged that Demian's mother was very rich. It was also said that she never went to church, and neither did her son. They were Jews, one rumor claimed, but they could also be secret Mohammedans. And then legends were told of Max Demian's bodily strength. It was certain he had terribly humiliated the strongest one in his class, who had challenged him to a fight and called him a coward by his refusal. Those who were there said that Demian had simply grabbed him by the neck with one hand and pressed firmly, then the boy became pale, and after that he crawled away and couldn't use his arm anymore for days. One evening it was even said that he was dead. Then for a while people had enough. Not much later, however, new rumors arose among us schoolchildren, who were aware of reports that Demian was on familiar terms with girls and "knew everything."

Meanwhile my affair with Franz Kromer continued its compulsory course. I was not free of him, for even when he left me alone for days in-between, I was still bound to him. In my dreams he lived along like my shadow, and what he did not do to me in reality, that my imagination allowed him to do in these dreams, in which I was absolutely his slave. I lived in these dreams — I have always been a great dreamer — more than in the actual, I lost strength and life on account of these dreams. Among other things, I often dreamed that Kromer mishandled me, that he spit on me and kneeled on me, and, what was worse, that he misled me into serious crime — not misled rather, but simply compelled through his powerful influence. The most frightful of these dreams, from which I awoke half insane, consisted of a murderous assault upon my father. Kromer sharpened a knife and handed it to me, we stood behind the trees in an alley and lay in wait for somebody, I knew not whom; but when somebody came along and Kromer put pressure on my arm to say he was the one whom I must stab, then it was my father. Then I awoke.

Due to these things I still well indeed thought about Cain and Abel, but little more about Demian. When he first stepped up to me again, it was, oddly enough, also in a dream. Namely, I dreamed once more of the ill-usage and forced violence which I suffered, but instead of Kromer it was Demian this time who kneeled on me. And — this was quite new and made a deep impression on me — all that I had suffered from Kromer amidst torture and opposition, this I suffered gladly from Demian with a feeling that consisted of just as much joy as anguish. This dream I had twice, then Kromer regained his place.

What I experienced in these dreams and what I experienced in reality, this I have not been able to exactly separate anymore for the longest time. In any case, however, my bad relationship with Kromer took its course, and was not nearly at an end, when at last I had paid off the indebted sum out of nothing but petty thieveries. No, now he knew of these thieveries, for he always asked me where the money came from, and I was more in his power than ever. Frequently he threatened to tell my father everything, and even then my anxiety was hardly so great as the profound regret at the fact that I had not done so myself from the beginning. Meanwhile, and as miserable as I was, I still did not regret everything, at least not always, and came to feel at times that everything had to be so. A destiny hung over me, and it was useless trying to break through it.

Presumably my parents suffered not a little under these conditions. An alien spirit had come over me, I no longer passed in our community, which had been so intimate and toward which a furious homesickness often overtook me as if toward a lost paradise. I was treated, especially by my mother, more like an invalid than a miscreant, but how things actually stood, I could best see from the behavior of my two sisters. In this behavior, which was very sparing and yet caused me endless misery, it clearly manifested itself that I was a kind of demoniac, who for his condition was more to be lamented than chided, in whom, whoever, evil had precisely yet taken its place! I felt that I was being prayed for otherwise than before, and felt the fruitlessness of this praying. The longing for alleviation, the desire for a rightful confession I often sensed ardently, and yet also felt beforehand that neither to my father nor my mother would I say and could I explain all things properly. I knew that it would be kindly appraised, that they would be very sparing of me, yes, pitying, but not quite understanding, and the whole thing would be seen as a kind of going off the rails, while it was surely fate.

I know that many will not believe a child of not yet eleven years to be capable of feeling thus. To these people I do not relate my business. I relate it to those who know mankind better. The grown-up, who has learned to transform a part of his feelings into thoughts, misses these thoughts in the child and supposes then that the experiences are not there either. Only seldom in my life, however, have I experienced and suffered so deeply as I did then.

One day it rained, I was ordered by my torturer to the Burgplatz, there I stood now and waited and burrowed with my feet in the wet chestnut leaves, that still fell continually from the black, dripping trees. I had no money, but I had put aside two pieces of cake and carried them with me, in order to at least be able to give Kromer something. I was long accustomed to standing and waiting for him in a corner somewhere, often a very long time, and I suffered it, as man suffers the unalterable.

Finally Kromer came. Today he didn't stay long. He gave me a few thumps in the ribs, laughed, took the cake from me, even offered me a moist cigarette, which I didn't take, and was friendlier than usual.

"Yes," he said in leaving, "just so I don't forget — next time you can bring along your sister, the older one. What's her name anyway?"

I didn't know what he was talking about, and gave no answer. I simply looked at him amazed.

"Don't you get it? You're to bring your sister with."

"Yes, Kromer, but that's not possible. I'm not allowed to, and there's no way she would come along either."

I was prepared for this, that once again it was only chicanery and a pretext. He often did it thus, demand something impossible, place me in terror, humiliate me and then gradually be easy to deal with. Then I had to buy myself off with some money or other gifts.

This time he was quite different. At my refusal he hardly became angry at all.

"Oh well," he said casually, "you can think it over. I'd like to get acquainted with your sister. It'll happen yet sometime. You simply take her along on a stroll, and then I show up."

When he was gone, some sense of his request suddenly dawned on me. I was still a complete child, but I knew reportedly that boys and girls, when they were somewhat older, could do some mysterious, scandalous, and forbidden things with each other. And now I should therefore — suddenly it became quite clear to me, how monstrous it was! My resolve, never to do this, stood immediately fixed. But what would happen then and how Kromer would revenge himself on me, on that I hardly dared to think. It was the start of a new martyrdom for me, it was not yet enough.

Comfortless I walked across the empty square, hands in my pockets. New torments, new slavery!

Then a fresh, deep voice called to me. I grew frightened and began to run. Someone ran after me, a hand grasped me softly from behind. It was Max Demian.

I gave myself up.

"Is it you?" I said uncertain. "You frightened me so!"

He looked at me, and never had his look been more that of a grownup, a superior and penetrating one, than now. For a long time we had not spoken to each other.

"I'm sorry," he said with his courteous and yet very decisive manner. "But listen, one mustn't let oneself be so frightened."

"Well yes, still it can happen."

"It seems so. But look: if you flinch that way in front of someone who has done nothing to you, then that someone begins to reflect. It surprises him, it makes him curious. That someone thinks to himself you are remarkably jumpy indeed, and he thinks further: so is one only, if one has fear. Cowards always have fear; but I believe you're not actually a coward. Isn't that true? Oh certainly, you're not a hero either. There are things you're afraid of; there are also men you're afraid of. And one should never have that. No, one should never be afraid of man. You're not afraid of me, are you? Or?"

"Oh no, not at all."

"Exactly, you see. But there are people you're afraid of?"

"I don't know... But let me be, what do you want from me?"

He kept pace with me. I had walked faster with thoughts of flight — and I felt his glance from the side toward me.

"Just suppose," he began, "that I mean you well. In any case you don't need to be afraid of me. I'd like to try an experiment with you, it will be fun and you can learn something besides which will prove very useful. Now pay attention! — Thus I sometimes attempt an art which is called mind-reading. There is no witchcraft connected with it, but if one does not know how it is done, then it appears quite peculiar. One can surprise people very much with it. — Now, let's give it a try. So I like you or I'm interested in you and now I want to bring out how things look inside you. I have already taken the first step toward that. I have given you a fright — you are therefore frightened. There are thus things and men that you fear. Where can that come from? You need not fear anyone. If you are afraid of somebody, then the reason is that you have allowed this somebody to have power over you. One has done something evil, and the other knows this — then he has power over you. You get it? It's quite clear, isn't it?"

I looked helplessly into his face, which was serious and intelligent as ever, and kindly too, but without any tenderness, it was severe rather. Righteousness or something similar lay therein. I was not aware how it happened to me; he stood like a sorcerer before me.

"Have you got it?" he asked once more.

I nodded. I could say nothing.

"I told you so, it appears comical, reading someone's mind, but it happens quite naturally. For example, I could pretty much tell you exactly what you thought about me that time when I told you the story of Cain and Abel. Well, that is beside the point. I also think it possible that you once dreamed about me. Let's leave that however! You're a sharp young man, most people are so stupid! I like talking now and then to a sharp young man, someone I can rely on. Are you all right with that?"

"Oh yes. Only I don't understand at all —"

"Let's stay with our amusing experiment for now! We have thus discov-ered: boy S. is frightened — he is afraid of someone — he probably shares a secret with this other person, which makes him very uneasy. — Is that about right?"

As though in a dream I succumbed to his voice, his influence. I merely nodded. Wasn't a voice speaking here that could only have come out of me? Which knew everything? Which knew everything better, clearer than me myself?

Strongly Demian clapped me on the shoulder.

"So that's right. I thought it might be. Now just one more question: do you know the name of the boy who left you back there?"

I was violently alarmed, my impugned secret wriggled back painfully into me, it didn't want to come to light.

"What sort of boy? There was no boy there, just me."

He laughed.

"Just tell me!" he laughed. "What's his name?"

I whispered: "Do you mean that Frantz Kromer?"

Satisfied he nodded at me.

"Bravo! You're a smart fellow, we'll become friends yet. But now I must tell you something: this Kromer, or whatever his name is, is a bad fellow. His face tells me that he is a rascal! What do you think?"

"Oh yes," I heaved a sigh, "he is bad, he is a Satan! But he must know nothing! For God's sake, he must know nothing! Do you know him? Does he know you?"

"Just take it easy! He's gone and he doesn't know me — not yet. But I'd be quite willing to make his acquaintance. He goes to public school?

"Yes."

"In which grade?"

"In the fifth. — But don't say anything to him! Please, please, don't say anything to him!"

"Be calm, nothing will happen to you. I presume you have no desire to tell a little more about this Kromer?"

"I can't! Let me be!"

He was silent for a while.

"Too bad," he said then, "we could have carried the experiment still further. But I don't want to pester you. But you know of course, don't you, that there's something not right about your fear of him? Such fear makes a complete wreck of us, one must free oneself of it. You must free yourself of it, if you mean to make a decent fellow out of yourself. You understand?"

"Certainly, you're quite right...but it's not possible. You just don't know..."

"You have seen that I know many a thing, more than you had thought. — Do you owe him some money?"

"Yes, that too, but that is not the main thing. I can't say it, I can't!"

"So it wouldn't help if I gave you enough to cover what you owe him? — I could easily give it to you."

"No, no that isn't it. And I beg you: don't tell anyone about it! Not a word! It'll be unfortunate for me."

"You can trust in me, Sinclair. Your secrets you can impart to me some time later —"

"Never, never!" I cried vehemently.

"Just as you like. I only mean, perhaps you will tell me more at some later time. Only voluntarily, it's understood! You don't think I'd act like Kromer himself, do you?"

"Oh no — but you know nothing at all about it!"

"Nothing at all. I merely thought about it. And I would never do it the way Kromer does it, that you can believe. You don't owe me anything, by the way."

We were quiet for a long time, and I became calmer. But Demian's knowledge became ever more puzzling to me.

"I'm going home now," he said and drew more fastly together in the rain his waterproof jacket. "I'd just like to say once more, since we've already come so far — you should get rid of this fellow! If there is no other way possible, then kill him! It would impress and please me if you did it. I would even help you."

I received new anxiety. The story of Cain suddenly struck me again. It made me uneasy, and I began softly to cry. Too much uneasiness was around me here.

"All right," smiled Max Demian. "Just go on home! We'll arrange things somehow. Although killing would be the simplest way. In such things the simplest is always the best. You are not in good hands with your friend Kromer."

I came home and it seemed to me that I had been away for a year. Everything looked different. Between me and Kromer stood something like a future, something like hope. I was no longer alone! And now I first saw how terribly alone I had been for weeks and weeks with my secret. And at once it struck me what I had reflected on many times: that a confession before my parents would relieve me but would definitely not redeem me completely. Now I had almost confessed, to another, to a stranger, and the notion of redemption flew towards me like a strong fragrance!!

All the same my anxiety was still not overcome for long, and I was still prepared for long and terrible clashes with my enemy. It was all the more remarkable to me that everything ran so quietly, so completely secret and peaceful.

Kromer's whistle failed to sound in front of our house, for a day, two days, three days, a week long. I didn't dare believe it and lay in wait inwardly, to see whether suddenly he would yet be standing there again, even if never ever expected. But he was gone and remained gone! Mistrustful towards this new freedom, I still thought it couldn't be right. Until finally one time I encountered Franz Kromer. He came down Seiler Lane straight towards me. When he saw me, he jerked all over, twisted his face into a wild grimace and turned around with no further ado, in order to avoid meeting me.

That was for me an unheard of moment! My foe ran away from me! My Satan was afraid of me! Joy and surprise ran through and through me.

In these days Demian showed himself once again. He waited for me in front of the school.

"Good day," I said.

"Good morning, Sinclair. I just wanted to hear how you're doing. Kromer isn't bothering you anymore, is he?"

"Is that your doing? But how then? How then? I don't understand it all. He's completely absent."

"That's good. If he should ever come around again — I don't think he will, but he is indeed a cheeky fellow — then simply tell him he might think about Demian."

"But how does all this hang together? Did you pick a quarrel with him and thrash him?"

"No, I'm not so keen on that. I simply spoke with him, just as I also did with you, and was able to make it clear to him that it was to his own advantage to leave you in peace."

"Oh, you will not have given him any money, I trust?"

"No, my boy. You already tried this route, didn't you?"

He disengaged himself, as much as I tried to ascertain by questioning him, and I was left behind with the old apprehensive feeling towards him that was strangely mixed with gratitude and shyness, admiration and anxiety, affection and inner resistance.

I intended to see him again soon, and then wanted to talk with him more about all this, about the Cain business as well.

It didn't happen.

Gratitude is generally not a virtue in which I believe, and to demand it of a child seems false to me. So I'm not exactly surprised at my own complete ingratitude toward Max Demian. I believe today with certainty that I would have been sick and ruined for life, had he not freed me from the clutches of Kromer. This liberation I already felt at that time too to be the greatest event of my young life — but the liberator himself I left lying there ignored as soon as he had performed his miracle.

As I said, ingratitude does not seem remarkable to me. Odd to me only is the lack of curiosity I displayed. How was it possible that I could go on living peacefully for a single day without coming nearer to the secrets with which Max Demian had brought me into contact? How could I restrain the craving to hear more about Cain, more about Kromer, more about mind-reading?

It is hardly conceivable, and yet it is so. I saw myself suddenly disentangled from demonic nets, saw once more the world lying before me bright and joyous, succumbed no more to anxiety attacks and suffocating heart palpitations. The spell was broken, I was tormented and damned no more, I was once again a schoolboy as always. My nature sought as quickly as possible to return to equilibrium and peace, and so it took all the pains to remove the many ugly and menacing things from itself, to forget them. Wonderfully fast the whole long story of my guilt and fright slipped my memory, without apparently having any scars and impressions left behind.

That on the other hand I just as quickly sought to forget my helper and savior, I understand today as well. From the vale of tears of my damnation, from the terrible slavery by Kromer I fled with all the instincts and powers of my injured soul back there, where I had been happy and content earlier: into the lost paradise that opened itself again, into the bright father- and mother- world, to my sisters, to the aroma of cleanliness, to the divine favor of Abel.

Already on the day after my short conversation with Demian when I was at last fully convinced of my regained freedom and no longer feared any relapses, I did that, which I so often and ardently had wished for — I confessed. I went to my mother, showed her the little savings box, whose hinge was damaged and which was filled with play money instead of real money, and I explained to her how for a long time I had been fettered through my own guilt to an evil tormentor. She didn't understand all of it, but she saw the box, she saw my transformed look, heard my transformed voice, felt that I was recovered, that I had been restored to her.

And now I celebrated with high spirits the feast of my re-admittance, the return of the Prodigal Son. Mother brought me to father, the story was repeated, questions and outcries of amazement crowded themselves in, both parents breathed sighs of relief at the long oppression. Everything was splendid, everything was as in the stories, everything dissolved into a wonderful harmony.

Into this harmony I now fled with true passion. I could not sate myself enough on it, the fact that I once more had my peace and the trust of my parents; I became a domestic model child, played more than ever with my sisters and sang along at devotions the dear, old songs with the feelings of one redeemed and converted.

Yet things were so very not in order! And here is the point from which my forgetfulness toward Demian is alone truly explained. To him I should have confessed! The confession would have been less decorative and stir-ring, but would have turned out more fruitful for me. Now I clung with all the roots to my former paradisiacal world, had returned home and was received in grace. Demian, however, in no way belonged to this world, he was not fit for it. He too was, different than Kromer, but even still — he too was a seducer, he too connected me with the second, the evil, bad world, and of that world I now wanted to forever know nothing more. I could not and would not now deliver up Abel and help glorify Cain, now, when I had just myself become an Abel again.

Thus the outward connection. The inner, however, was this: I was delivered out of Kromer's and the devil's hands, but not through my own strength and doing. I had attempted to wander on the paths of the world, and they had been too slippery for me. Well, then the grip of a friendly hand had saved me, I ran, without more than a side-glance, back into the lap of my mother and the security of a fenced-in, pious childishness. I made myself younger, more dependent than I was. I had to replace the dependence on Kromer with a new one, for I was not capable of going it alone. So I chose, in the blindness of my heart, the dependence on father and mother, on the old beloved "world of light," of which I already knew though that it wasn't the only world. Had I not done this, then I would have had to hold out with Demian and entrust myself to him. That I did not do this appeared to me at the time as justified mistrust toward his odd ideas; in truth it was nothing other than fear. For Demian would have demanded more from me than my parents demanded, much more, he would have tried to make me more independent with incitement and admonition, with mockery and irony. Ah, this I know today: nothing is more repugnant to man than to go down the path that leads him to himself!

Nevertheless, perhaps half a year later, I could not resist the temptation and asked during a stroll with my father, what was to be made of the fact that many people declared Cain to be better than Abel.

He was very surprised and explained to me that this was a reading that lacked novelty. It had already appeared even in early Christian times and had been taught to sects, one of which was called the "Cainites." But naturally this crazy teaching was nothing other than an attempt by the devil to destroy our faith. For if one believed in the right of Cain and the wrong of Abel, then it follows as a consequence that God had erred, that thus the God of the Bible was not the right and only one, but a false one. Actually the Cainites had taught and preached something similar: of course this heresy had long since vanished from humanity and he wondered only that a comrade of mine from school could have come to know something about it. Nevertheless he warned me seriously to leave off these thoughts.

CHAPTER THREE. THE THIEF

It would be a fine, tender, and lovable thing to tell of my childhood, of my being in safety with father and mother, of filial love and a contented playful passing of life in gentle, dear, light surroundings. But I am interested only in the steps that I took in my life to arrive at myself. All the pretty resting points, islands of happiness and paradises, whose charm was not unknown to me, I let lie in the splendor of the distance and do not desire to set foot there anymore.

Therefore I speak, so long as I still tarry with my time of boyhood, only of what new things came to me, what drove me forwards, tore me loose.

Always came these impulses from the "other world," always they brought anxiety, constraint, and a bad conscience with them, always they were revolutionary and endangered the peace in which I gladly would have remained living.

Then came the years in which I had to discover anew that an original drive existed in me which in the lawful and light world had to crawl away and conceal itself. As with every man, so I too was assailed by the slowly awakening feeling of sexuality as an enemy and destroyer, as a forbidden thing, as temptation and sin. What my curiosity sought, what dreams, desire and anxiety created for me, the great mystery of puberty, that didn't pass at all in the fenced-in blissfulness of my childhood peace. I did as all do. I led the double life of a child, who is no longer indeed a child. My consciousness lived in the homely and lawful, my consciousness denied the upward-dawning new world. Beside that, however, I lived in dreams, drives, wishes of a subterranean kind, across which that conscious life built ever more anxious bridges, for the childhood world in me had fallen apart. Like almost all parents, so mine too were of no help with the awakening life impulses, of which nothing was to be spoken. They helped only, with inexhaustible care, my hopeless attempts to deny reality and further reside in a children's world that had become ever more unreal and untruthful. I don't know whether parents can do much herein, and place no blame on mine. It was my own affair, with me to settle and my way to find, and I managed things badly, like most well-bred types.

Every man lives through this difficulty. For the average man this is the point in life where the demands of his own life come hardest into conflict with the environment, where the way forwards must be most bitterly gained by struggle. Many experience the dying and being reborn that is our fate only this one time in their life, with a becoming rotten and giving way of childhood, when everything that has become dear wants to forsake us and we suddenly feel the loneliness and deadly cold of the universe around us. And very many remain hanging on this cliff forever and cleave their whole life long painfully to an irretrievable past, to the dream of a lost paradise, which is the worst and most murderous of all dreams.

Let us turn back to the story. The sensations and dream images, in which the end of childhood announced itself to me, are not important enough to be related. The important thing was: the "dark world," the "other world" was here again. What Franz Kromer once had been, that was now stuck fast in me. And with that too from outside hither the "other world" had regained power over me.

Several years had passed since the story with Kromer. That dramatic and guilt-filled time of my life lay very distant from me and seemed like a brief nightmare that had faded into nothing. Franz Kromer had long since vanished from my life, so that I hardly took note whenever I happened to meet him. The other important figure of my tragedy, however, Max Demian, no longer vanished completely from my circle. It is true he stood far on the edge for a long time, visible, but not effective. Only gradually did he tread nearer again, radiating strength and influence again.

I search myself to recollect what I knew about Demian at the time. It may be that for a year or longer I did not speak to him one single time. I avoided him, and he in no way pressed himself on me. Perhaps once, when we happened upon each other, he nodded to me. At times then it seemed to me there was in his friendliness a fine tone of scorn or ironical reproach, but it may have been my imagination. The history that I had experienced with him, and the strange influence he had exercised upon me then, were as if forgotten, from him as well as from me.

I search for his figure, and well, when I reflect on him, I see that he was there indeed and noted by me. I see him on his way to school, alone or amongst several other older students, and I see him kind of strange, solitary and quiet, as though wandering starrily, surrounded by his own atmosphere, living under his own laws. Nobody loved him, nobody was on familiar terms with him, only his mother, and even with her he seemed to carry on not like a child but like a grown-up. The teachers left him in the greatest possible peace, he was a good student, but he sought to please no one, and now and then we heard according to report of some word, a snide remark or reply that he was supposed to have made to a teacher and which in brusque challenge and irony left nothing to be desired.

I recollect, with closed eyes, and I see his image emerge. Where was that? Yes, there it is again now. It was in the alley before our house. I saw him standing there one day, notebook in hand, and saw him drawing. He was drawing the old heraldic figure with the bird. And I stood at a window hidden behind the curtain, and watched him, and saw with profound astonishment his attentive, cool, clear countenance turned toward the coat of arms, the countenance of a man, of a scientist or an artist, superior and replete with will, singularly clear and cool, with knowing eyes.

And again I see him. It was a little later, on the street; we all stood, having come from school, around a horse that had fallen. It lay, still harnessed to the shaft, in front of a farmer's wagon, snorted searchingly and plaintively with dilated nostrils into the air and bled from an imperceptible wound, so that on his side the white street dust had slowly and fully sucked up dark. As I, with a feeling of nausea, turned away from the sight, I saw Demian's face. He had not forced his way to the front, he stood at the very back, at ease and quite elegant, as was suitable to him. His glance seemed directed on the horse's head and had again this deep, silent, almost fanatical and yet dispassionate attentiveness. I was obliged to look at him a long time, and then I felt, still far from consciousness, something very peculiar. I saw Demian's face, and I saw not only that he had no boy's face, but that of a man; I saw even more, I believed I saw, or sensed, that it wasn't the face of a man either, but still something else. It was as though there was also something of a woman's face therein, and in particular this face seemed to me, for a moment, neither manly nor childlike, neither old nor young, but a thousand years old, somehow timeless, stamped by other conjunctures than those we live. Animals could look thus, or trees, or stars — I didn't know that, I didn't exactly feel that which I'm now saying as a grownup about it, but something similar. Perhaps he was handsome, perhaps he pleased me, perhaps he was also repellent to me, that too was not to be decided. I saw only this: he was different from us, he was like an animal, or like a spirit, or like a picture, I don't know what he was like, but he was different, unimaginably different from us all.

More the memory does not say to me, and perhaps this too is already in part derived from later impressions.

Only when I was several years older did I finally come into closer contact again with him. Demian was not, as custom demanded, confirmed with his age group, and thereby was immediately again also connected with rumors. It was said in the school again that he was actually a Jew, or no, a heathen, and others knew that, together with his mother, he was without any religion or belonged to a fabulous, evil sect. In connection with that I think I also heard he was suspected of living with his mother as though with a lover. Presumably it was such that he had hitherto been brought up without a creed, that this now, however, allowed for some unwholesome fears concerning his future. At any rate his mother determined, now at least, two years later than his contemporaries, to let him take part in Confirmation. So it came about that he was now my month-long comrade in Confirmation instruction.

For a while I held back from him completely, I wanted to have no part of him, there were all too many rumors and secrets surrounding him for me; particularly disturbing to me, however, was the feeling of obligation that since the affair with Kromer had remained behind in me. And precisely at that time I had enough to do with my own secrets. For me Confirmation instruction coincided with decisive enlightenments in sexual matters, and despite good intentions my interest in the pious teaching was greatly impaired thereby. The things of which the clergyman spoke lay far away from me in a quiet, holy unreality; they were perhaps quite beautiful and valuable, but in no way actual and exciting, and those other things were precisely this in the highest degree.

The more now this condition made me indifferent to my instruction, the more my interest drew me near to Max Demian again. Something or other seemed to bind us. I must trace this thread as exactly as possible. As far as I can remember, it began at an hour early in the morning when the light was still burning in our schoolroom. Our spiritual instructor had come to the story of Cain and Abel. I hardly paid attention to it, I was sleepy and hardly listened. Then the parson in an elevated tone began to speak affectingly about the mark of Cain. At this moment I sensed a kind of touching or warning, and looking up I saw from the front row of benches the face of Demian turned back toward me, with a bright, eloquent eye, whose expression could just as well be mocking as serious. He looked at me only for a moment, and suddenly I listened intently to the parson's words, heard him talk about Cain and his mark, and sensed deep inside me a knowledge that it was not as he taught it, that one could also look at it differently, that criticism was possible about it!

In this minute there was once again a bond between Demian and me. And strange — hardly was this feeling of a certain belonging-together in the soul there when I saw it as if magically carried over into the spatial as well. I didn't know whether he could arrange it so himself or whether it was pure chance — at the time I still firmly believed in chance events — after a few days Demian had suddenly changed his seat in the religion hour and sat right in front of me (I still recall how readily in the midst of the wretched poorhouse-inhabitant air of the overfilled schoolroom in the morning I imbibed here the tender, fresh scent of soap from his neck!), and again after a few days he had changed again and now sat next to me, and there he remained sitting, the whole winter and throughout the whole spring.

The morning hours had changed completely. They were no longer sleepy and boring. I looked forward to them. Sometimes we both listened to the parson with the utmost attention, a glance from my neighbor was enough to point out for me a remarkable story, a strange saying. And another glance from him, quite determined, was enough to admonish me, to stir up criticism and doubt in me.

Very often, however, we were bad students and heard nothing of our instruction. Demian was always polite towards the teacher and our fellow students, I never saw him engage in schoolboy pranks, never heard of him laughing loudly or chattering, he never incurred censure from a teacher. But altogether quietly, and more with signs and looks than with words of whisper, he knew how to let me take part in his own occupations. These were in part of a strange nature.

He said to me, for instance, which students interested him, and in what manner he studied them. Many he knew very precisely. He said to me before the lesson: "When I give you a sign with my thumb, then so and so will turn around and look at us, or scratch his neck," and so on. During the hour then, when I often had hardly thought anymore thereon, suddenly Max would turn toward me with a striking gesture of his thumb; I quickly scouted out the indicated student and saw him each time, as if pulled by a wire, perform the desired gesture. I pestered Max to try it on the teacher one time too, but he would not do so. But one time when I came into class and said to him that I had not done my assignment that day and hoped very much that the parson would not ask me anything today, then he did help me. The parson searched for a student whom he would allow to recite some part of the catechism, and his roaming eye remained stuck on my guilt-conscious face. Slowly he approached, extended his finger toward me, already had my name on his lips — then he became suddenly distracted or ill at ease, pulled at his shirt collar, stepped up to Demian, who looked him straight in the face, appeared to want to ask him something, turned away again surprisingly, coughed for a while and then called on a different student.

Only gradually did I notice, while these jests amused me very much, that my friend frequently played the same game with me. It happened that on the way to school I suddenly had the feeling Demian was behind me a stretch and when I turned he was right there.

"Can you actually make someone think what you want him to?" I asked him.

He gave the information willingly, calm and factual, in his grownup manner.

"No," he said, "that no one can do. We have no free will namely, even if the parson pretends we do. A person can neither think what he wants, nor can I make him think what I want. But to be sure one can observe somebody well, and then one can often say pretty exactly what he thinks or feels, and then one can mostly predict what he will do in the next moment. It's quite simple, people just don't know it. Naturally it takes practice. There is, for example, among the butterflies a certain night moth, among which the females are much rarer than the males. The moths propagate exactly as do all animals, the male fertilizes the female — it is often tested by naturalists — then in the night the male moths come to these females, and in fact from hours away! Hours away, just think! One attempts to explain this, but it is difficult. It must be their sense of smell or some such thing, perhaps the way a good hunting dog can find and follow after an imperceptible track. Do you understand? These are the kinds of things that Nature is full of, and no one can explain them. Now I say however: if among these butterflies the females were as abundant as the males, the latter would just not have the fine nose! They have it simply because they have trained themselves thereon. When an animal or a man fixes his whole attention and his whole will on one definite thing, then he attains it as well. That is all. And it is exactly so with what you suggest. Look at a man exactly enough, then you will know more about him than he himself does."

It was on the tip of my tongue to utter the word "mind-reading" and with that remind him of the scene with Kromer, which lay so long in the past. But this was now also a strange matter between the two of us: never and at no time did either he or I make the slightest allusion thereupon, that once several years earlier he had so seriously intervened in my life. It was as if there had never been anything between us earlier, or as if each of us firmly reckoned that the other had forgotten it. Once or twice it even happened that we were walking down the street and came upon Franz Kromer, but we exchanged no glance, spoke no word about him.

"But what is all this with the will now?" I asked. "You say, one has no free will. But then again you say, one need only firmly fix his will upon something, then he can attain his goal. It doesn't add up though! If I am not the master of my will, then I certainly cannot direct my will here or there as I please either."

He clapped me on the shoulder. He always did that when I made him happy.

"Good that you ask!" he said, laughing. "One must always ask, one must always doubt. But the matter is quite simple. If a night-moth were to try to direct his will upon a star or some other such place, then it couldn't do this. Only — it would never attempt that at all. It seeks only that which has sense and value for it, what it needs, what it absolutely must have. And precisely thereby it also succeeds in achieving the incredible — it develops a magical sixth sense, that no creature outside it has! Our kind has more scope, certainly, and more interests than an animal. But we too are bounded in a proportionately very narrow compass and cannot get out beyond it. I can well indulge this and that fantasy, perhaps imagine to myself I absolutely want to go to the North Pole, or some such thing, but to carry it out and want it strongly enough, I can only do that if the wish lies completely in me myself, if in reality my whole being is completely filled up with it. Once that is the case, once you probe something which has been commanded forth from inside you, then it works too, then you can harness your will like a good nag. If for example I were to propose now to want to bring about that our parson henceforth wore glasses no more, then that wouldn't work. That would be mere foolery. But when I, back in the fall, had the firm intention to change my place there on the bench to the front, then it went quite well. There was suddenly someone there, who came before me in the alphabet, and who had been sick hith-erto, and because somebody had to make room for him, I was naturally the one who did it, because precisely my will was prepared to seize the opportunity at once."

"Yes," I said, "for me at the time it was also quite peculiar. From that moment on, when we took an interest in each other, you moved ever nearer to me. But how did that come to be? In the beginning you didn't sit right next to me though, first you sat a few times on the bench there in front of me, wasn't it? How did that come about?"

"It was like this: I myself didn't quite know where I wanted to go when I desired to be gone from my first place. I only knew that I wanted to sit farther in the back. It was my will to come to you, but I was not yet conscious of it. At the same time your own will drew along and helped me. Only when I sat there in front of you did it occur to me that my wish was only half fulfilled — I noted that I had actually desired nothing other than to sit next to you."

"But at the time no new student had entered."

"No, but at the time I simply did what I wanted and sat down without hesitation next to you. The boy with whom I exchanged seats was merely surprised and let me do as I pleased. And the parson once noted to be sure that there had been a change there — in general, every time he has dealings with me something secretly annoys him, namely, he knows my name is Demian and that it's not right that I with my D last name should sit all the way back there with the S's. But that does not penetrate into his consciousness, because my will is against it and because I hinder him in it again and again. He only notices again and again that something is not right, and looks at me and begins to study it, the good gentleman. But I have a simple remedy for that. I look him very, very firmly in the eye every time. Very few people can tolerate that. They all become uneasy. If you want to attain something from someone and you look him unexpectedly very firmly in the eye, and he doesn't become uneasy, then give it up! You will attain nothing by him, never! But that happens very seldom. I know actually only one single person with whom it doesn't help me."

"Who is that?" I asked quickly.

He looked at me with the somewhat diminished eyes which he got upon reflection. Then he looked away and gave no answer, and I, despite fervent curiosity, could not repeat the question.

I believe, however, that he was speaking then of his mother. — With her he seemed to live very intimately, but never spoke to me about her, never took me home with him. I hardly knew what his mother looked like.

Sometimes in those days I made attempts to do things like him and so draw together my will on something that I was bound to attain it. There were wishes there that seemed pressing enough to me. But it was nothing and went nowhere. I could not bring myself to speak with Demian about it. What I would have wished for myself, I could not have confessed to him. And he did not ask either.

My devoutness in questions of religion had in the meantime developed many gaps. But I differentiated myself, in my thoroughly Demian-influenced thoughts, very much from those of my fellow students, who exhibited complete unbelief. There were a few such ones, and they let slip occasional words like that it was ridiculous and unworthy of man to believe in a God and that stories like those of the Trinity and of Jesus' virgin birth were simply a joke, and that it was a disgrace that people today were still going around peddling this rubbish. I in no way thought thus. Even where I had doubts, I knew for sure from the whole experience of my childhood enough of the reality of a pious life, as my parents, for instance, led it, and that this was neither something unworthy nor dissembled. On the contrary, I had towards the religious the deepest reverence. Demian had just accustomed me to look at and interpret the narratives and religious dogma more freely, personally, playfully, and imaginatively; at least I followed the interpretations, which he explained to me, always gladly and with pleasure. Many things of course were too rough for me, such as the business concerning Cain. And once during Confirmation instruction he startled me with a conception which was if possible more daring yet. The teacher had been speaking about Golgotha. The Biblical account of the passion and death of the Savior had made a deep impression upon me since my earliest years; sometimes as a little boy, perhaps on Good Friday, after the time that my father had read aloud the Passion story, intimately and affectedly I lived in this sorrowful-beautiful, pale, ghostly and yet tremendously alive world, in Gethsemane and on Golgotha, and upon listening to Bach's *St Matthew's Passion* the gloomy, powerful suffering glow of this mystery-filled world with all its mystical shudders had inundated me. Even today I find in this music, and in the *Actus Tragicus*, the epitome of all poesy and all artistic expression.

Now at the end of that hour Demian said pensively to me: "There's something there, Sinclair, which doesn't please me. Read the story once more and test it on your tongue to see if there isn't something there that tastes off. Namely the thing with the two thieves. Magnificent how the three crosses stand there next to each other on the hill! But then this sentimental little tractate story with the honest thief! First he was a criminal and committed shameful acts, God knows what all, and now he melts away there and celebrates such a tearful feast of betterment and remorse! What sense is it to have such remorse two steps away from the grave, I ask you? It is once again nothing other than a righteous parson's tale, sickly-

sweet and dishonest with schmaltz of emotion and the highest edifying
background. If today you had to choose one of the two thieves as a friend
or consider which of the two you would rather put your trust in, then it is
certainly not at all this tearful convert. No, it's the other one, he is a manly
fellow and has character. He doesn't care a straw about conversion, which
indeed in his situation can only just be a pretty speech, he goes his way to
the end and says nothing cowardly in his last moment to absolve himself
of the devil, who has had to help him hitherto. He has character, and the
people with character in the Bible gladly get the worst of it. Perhaps he is
even a descendant of Cain. Don't you think so?"

I was very confounded. Here in the Crucifixion story I had believed
myself to be quite at home and only now saw how little personally, with
how little power of representation and imagination I had listened to
it and read it. Yet Demian's newer thinking sounded odious to me and
threatened to overthrow concepts in me upon whose steadfast existence
I believed I had to hold. No, one could not just go changing each and every
thing, even the most sacred.

He took notice of my resistance, as always, immediately, even before I
had said anything whatsoever.

"I already know," he said, "it's the same old story. Just don't take it seriously! But I want to tell you something — : here is one of those points
where we can very clearly see the lack in this religion. The point is that
this whole God, both Old and New Testament, is to be sure an outstanding
figure, but not that which he is nevertheless actually supposed to represent. He is the good, the noble, the fatherly, the beautiful and sublime
as well, the sentimental — quite right! But the world consists of something else besides. And all that is now simply ascribed to the devil, and
this entire part of the world, this entire half is suppressed and hushed
up — exactly how they praise God as the father of all life, but the entire
sex life, upon which life rests, after all, is simply hushed up and wherever
possible explained as devilish tricks and sinful! I have nothing against
people revering this God Jehovah, not the least bit. But I think we should
revere and hold sacred all things, the entire world, not only this artificially
separated, official half! So next to the divine service we must also then
have a devil's service. That I would find correct. Or else we would have
to create for ourselves a God who also comprised the devil in himself, and

before which we would not have to close our eyes when the most natural things in the world happen."

Opposed to his usual style, he almost became vehement, yet right after that he smiled and pressed me no further.

In me, however, these words hit upon the riddle of my whole boyhood years, which I carried in me every hour and of which I had never said a word to anybody. What Demian had said there about God and the devil, about the godly-official and the hushed-up devilish one, that was just precisely my own thought, my own myth, the thought of the two worlds or world-halves — the light and the dark. The insight that my problem was a problem of all men, a problem of all living and thinking, suddenly flew over me like a holy shadow, and anguish and reverence came over me, when I saw and suddenly felt, how deeply my most special, personal life and thinking had a part in the eternal stream of great ideas. The insight was not joyous, although somehow confirming and gratifying. It was hard and tasted raw, because a sound of responsibility lay in it, of no longer being allowed to be a child, of standing alone.

Revealing such a deep secret for the first time in my life, I told my comrade of the conception extant since my earliest childhood days of the "two worlds," and he saw immediately that my deepest feeling accorded and agreed with his. But it was not his nature to make use of things this way. He listened with deeper attentiveness, than he had ever given me before, and looked into my eyes until I had to avert mine. Then I saw in his gaze again that strange, animalistic timelessness, that unimaginable age.

"We'll talk more about it another time," he said, sparing me. "I see that you think more than you can express. If that is now so, then you also know, however, that you have never quite lived the life you thought, and that is not good. Only the thought that we are alive has any value. You have known that your 'allowed world' was only half the world, and you have tried to suppress the second half the way priests and teachers do. You will not succeed! No one succeeds in this once he has begun thinking."

It struck me deeply.

"But," I almost shrieked, "there are real and actual wicked and forbidden things, that you certainly cannot deny! And they are simply forbidden, and we must renounce them. I know of course that there is murder and all possible vices, but shall I then, merely because they exist, go out and become a criminal?"

"We won't be finished with this today," Max said soothedly. "You certainly shouldn't murder or rape and kill girls for pleasure, no. But you aren't yet at the point where one can perceive what 'allowed' and 'forbidden' actually means. You have only scented a piece of the truth. The other is yet to come, you can depend on it! You have had now, for example, for perhaps a year, a drive in you which is stronger than all others, and it is considered 'forbidden'. The Greeks and many other peoples, on the contrary, made this drive into a deity and honored him in great feasts. 'Forbidden' is thus nothing eternal, it can change. Even today of course anyone can sleep with a woman as soon as he has been to the pastor with her and has married her. With other peoples it is different, even today still. That is why each one of us has to find out for himself what is allowed and what is forbidden — forbidden to him. A person can never do a thing forbidden and can be a great rascal at the same time. And just as well vice-versa. — Actually it's only a question of convenience! He who is too comfortable to think for himself and be his own judge, he accommodates himself precisely to the prohibitions as they now stand. He has it easy. Others scent out laws in themselves, to them some things are forbidden, which every man of honor does daily, and there are other things allowed them which are otherwise forbidden. Each person must stand on his own two feet."

He suddenly seemed to regret having said so much and broke off. Already at that time I could identify to some degree with the feeling he was experiencing thereby. As pleasantly and seemingly superficial as he was wont namely to bring forth his sudden ideas, he certainly could not abide conversation "only for the sake of talking," as he once said, to the point of death. With me, however, he sensed, next to genuine interest, too much play, too much joy in clever chit-chat, or something akin, in short, a lack of complete seriousness.

As I reread the last words that I wrote — "complete seriousness" — , another scene suddenly strikes me again, the most impressive that I experienced in those yet half-childlike times.

Our Confirmation was drawing near, and the last hours of our spiritual instruction dealt with The Last Supper. This was important to the pastor and he took pains about it, something of consecration and elation could well be perceived in these hours. Only precisely then my thoughts were tied up with something else, and truly it was with the person of my friend. While I awaited the Confirmation which was explained to us as the solemn adoption into the community of the Church, the thought urgently pressed itself upon me that for me the value of this half-year or so of religious instruction lay not in what we had learned here, but in the nearness and the influence of Demian. Not in the Church was I now ready to be taken up, but into something quite different, into an order of thinking and of personality which had to exist somewhere on earth and whose representative and messenger I took to be my friend.

I sought to repress these thoughts, I was serious about experiencing the solemnity of the Confirmation with a certain dignity, in spite of everything, and this seemed to little agree with my new thoughts. Though I might do what I wanted, the thought was there, and it gradually attached itself with that of the imminent church celebration; I was ready to celebrate it differently from the others, it was to mean for me the acceptance into a world of thought as I had come to know it in Demian.

It was in those days that I once more had a lively dispute with him; it was just before our instruction hour. My friend was reserved and took no joy in my speaking, which was no doubt pretty precocious and pompous.

"We talk too much," he said with unaccustomed seriousness. "Clever speech has no value at all, none at all. One only loses oneself. To lose oneself is a sin. One must be able to fully crawl inside oneself like a tortoise."

Right after that we entered the school room. The lesson began, I took pains to pay attention, and Demian didn't disturb me in this. After a while I began to sense on the side there, where he sat next to me, something peculiar, an emptiness or coolness or something like that, as though the seat had unexpectedly become vacant. As the feeling began to grow constraining, I turned around to look.

There I saw my friend sitting, upright and with good bearing as usual. But nevertheless he looked completely different than usual, and something emanated from him, something enveloped him, what I did not know. I believed he had his eyes shut, but saw that they were open. They were not looking, however, they were unseeing, they were fixed and turned inward or off into a great distance. Perfectly motionless he sat there, he didn't seem to breathe either, his mouth was as though carved out of wood or stone. His face was pale, uniformly wan, like stone, and his brown hair was the most living thing about him. His hands lay before him on the bench, lifeless and still like objects, like stones or fruit, wan and motion-less, yet not slack, but like solid, good husks around a hidden, strong life.

The sight made me tremble. He is dead! I thought, almost saying it aloud. But I knew that he was not dead. I hung with a spellbound look on his face, on this pale, stony mask, and I felt: this is Demian! How he was otherwise, when he walked and talked with me, that was only a half of Demian, one who temporarily played a role, one who adapted himself, who went along out of complaisance. The real Demian, however, looked like this, just like this, so stony, primeval, animal-like, stone-like, beau-tiful and cold, dead and secretly filled with unheard-of life. And around him here this still emptiness, this aether and starry space, this lonely death!

Now he is gone completely into himself, I felt among shudders. Never had I been so isolated. I took no part in him, he was inaccessible to me, he was farther from me than if he had been on the most distant island in the world.

I hardly conceived that no one outside of me could see it! Everyone should have looked here, everyone should have shuddered! But no one paid attention to him. He sat statue-like, and, I would have to think, stiff as an idol, a fly settled on his forehead and made its way slowly across his nose and lips — he didn't move a muscle.

Where, where was he now? What was he thinking, what was he feeling? Was he in a heaven, was he in a hell?

It was not possible for me to ask him about it. When I saw him, at the end of the hour, living and breathing again, when I met his gaze, he was as earlier. Where did he come from? Where had he been? He seemed tired. His face had color again, his hands moved again, but his brown hair was now lustreless and as though fatigued.

In the days that followed I devoted myself in my bedroom many times to a new exercise: I would sit straight up in a chair, make my eyes glassy, keep completely motionless and wait to see how long I could hold out and what I would experience thereby. Yet I only grew weary and my eyelids itched furiously.

Soon afterwards was Confirmation, about which I have no important recollections.

Now everything changed. My childhood fell apart in ruins around me. My parents looked at me with a certain embarrassment. My sisters became quite estranged from me. A disenchantment made false and pale my usual feelings and joys, the garden was without fragrance, the wood had no allure, the world stood around me like a clearance sale of old goods, flat and unattractive, books were paper, music was noise. Thus falls the leaf down from an autumnal tree, he feels it not, rain runs down on him, or sun, or frost, and in him life retracts slowly into the narrowest and innermost place. He doesn't die. He waits.

It was determined that after summer vacation I should be sent off to another school and be way from home for the first time. At times my mother would approach me with particular tenderness, taking leave beforehand, intent on conjuring love, homesickness, and unforgettableness in my heart. Demian was away on a trip. I was alone.

Chapter Four. Beatrice

Without having seen my friend again, I traveled at the end of my vacation to St. _____. Both my parents came along and gave me over with all possible care to the protection of a boy's pension run by a teacher at the gymnasium. They would have been petrified with horror if they had known into what kind of things they were now letting me wander.

The question was still whether in time I could become a good son and useful citizen, or whether my nature would push me along on other roads. My last attempt at happiness, in the shadow of the paternal house and spirit, had lasted a long time, had nearly succeeded for a time, and yet had completely foundered in the end.

The strange emptiness and isolation, which I came to feel for the first time during vacation after my Confirmation (how I learned later yet to recognize it, this emptiness, this thin air!), did not pass so quickly. The departure from home was strangely easy, I was actually ashamed that I was not more melancholy, my sisters wept for no reason, I could not cry. I was astounded at myself. I had always been a sentimental child and fundamentally a pretty good child. Now I was completely transformed. I was utterly indifferent toward the outside world and spent days only concerned with hearkening to what was inside me and hearing the streams, the forbidden and dark streams that subterraneously rushed there in me. I had grown very rapidly, only in the last half year, and looked gangly, meager, and unfinished in the world. The loveableness of the boy had completely disappeared from me; I myself felt that no one could love me thus, and I in no way loved myself either. Toward Max Demian I often had a great longing; but not seldom I also hated him and blamed him for the impoverishment of my life, which I took upon myself like an ugly sickness.

In our boarding school I was neither loved nor esteemed in the beginning; at first I was made a fool of, then they drew back from me and saw in me a hypocrite and an unpleasant eccentric. I took pleasure in the role, overdid it even, and ill-willed myself into a solitariness which on the outside looked continually like the manliest world contempt, whereas secretly I was often overcome by consuming attacks of pensive melancholy and despair. In school I managed to survive on the accumulated knowledge from back home, the class was somewhat behind compared to my earlier ones, and I accustomed myself to looking at my contemporaries somewhat contemptuously as children.

A year and longer it went on like this, even the first vacation visits home brought forth no new sounds; I gladly went away again.

It was the beginning of November. I had grown accustomed to taking short, thought-provoking walks in all weathers, upon which I often enjoyed a kind of rapture, a rapture full of melancholy, world-contempt, and self-contempt. Thus I strode one evening in the moist, foggy twilight through the surroundings of the town, the broad avenue of a public park stood completely deserted and invited me, the way lay thickly full with fallen leaves, in which I rummaged with my feet with dark voluptuousness, it smelled moist and bitter, the distant trees stepped forth ghostly-large and shadowy out of the misting.

At the end of the avenue I remained standing irresolutely, stared into the black foliage and breathed with eagerness the wet aroma of decomposition and decay, to which something in me responded and welcomed. O how stale life tasted!

Out of a by-way a man in a flowing mantle with cape came along, I wanted to go on walking, then he called to me.

"Hello, Sinclair!"

He came near, it was Alphonse Beck, the oldest one in our pension. I was always glad to see him and had nothing against him, except that with me as with all the younger ones he was always ironic and avuncular. He was reputed to be strong as a bear, said to have the master of our pension under his thumb, and was the hero of many grammar schoolboy rumors.

"What are you doing here then?" he cried affably in that tone the bigger ones had when they deigned on occasion to address one of us. "Well, shall we bet you're making up poetry?"

"Never entered my head," I brusquely refused.

He burst out laughing, walked next to me, and chattered in a manner I was no longer accustomed to at all.

"You need have no fear, Sinclair, that perhaps I do not understand this. It has something to do with when one is walking along thus at night in the fog, with autumnal thoughts and such, then one readily composes poems, this I know. On dying nature, naturally, and on lost youth, which it resembles. See Heinrich Heine."

"I'm not so sentimental," I said in my defense.

"Well, never mind then! But in this weather it seems to me a man would do well to seek a quiet place where a glass of wine or the like could be had. You want to come along for a bit? I'm quite alone just now — Or don't you care to? I wouldn't want to be your tempter, in case you should have to be a paragon of youth."

Soon thereafter we were sitting in a small suburban bar, drinking dubious wine and clinking thick glasses. At first it pleased me little, yet it was something new. Soon, however, unaccustomed to the wine, I became very talkative. It was as though a window in me was shoved open, the world shone therein — how long, how frightfully long had I not spoken from my soul. I indulged in reveries and in the midst therein as a treat I related the story of Cain and Abel!

Beck listened to me with pleasure — at last, somebody to whom I could give something! He clapped me on the shoulder, he called me a devilish fellow and my heart swelled high up with ecstasy, letting pent-up needs for speech and communication riotously stream forth, to be acknowledged and count for something with an older person. When he called me an ingenious rogue, the words ran like a sweet, strong wine into my soul. The world burned with new colors, thoughts flowed toward me from a hundred bold sources, spirit and fire blazed in me. We spoke about teachers and comrades, and it seemed to me we understood each other splendidly. We spoke of the Greeks and of heathendom, and Beck by all means wanted me to bring forth confessions about my love-adventures. I could not say a word at the time. I had no experience, nothing to relate. And what in me I had felt, construed, imagined, that sat burning in me to be sure but was also not loosened and made communicable by the wine. About girls Beck knew much more, and I listened ardently to these tales. Incredible things I came to know there, things never deemed possible trod into plain reality, seemed a matter of course. Alphonse Beck with his perhaps eighteen years had already amassed experiences. Among others this, that the thing with girls was they wanted nothing but flirting and gallantry, and that was indeed quite nice, but certainly not the real thing. In that case one could hope for more success with women. Women were much more sensible. For example, Mrs. Jaggelt, who had the store with the schoolbooks and pencils, with her one could talk business, and surely all the things that took place behind her counter would go in no book.

I sat deeply enchanted and stupefied. Of course I couldn't exactly love Mrs. Jaggelt — but all the same it was outrageous. There seemed to be sources flowing there, at least for the older boys, of which I had never dreamed. A false tone accompanied it for sure, and it all tasted meaner and more commonplace than in my opinion love ought to taste, — but still it was reality, it was love and adventure, there sat someone next to me who had experienced it, to whom it seemed a matter of course.

Our conversations went down a little, they had lost something. I was no longer the ingenious little fellow, I was now merely still a boy listening to a man. But nonetheless — compared to that which my life had been for months and months, this was precious, this was paradise. Moreover it was, as I only gradually began to feel, forbidden, strictly forbidden — from sitting in the bar to what we discussed. To me, at any rate, it smacked of spirit, it smacked of revolution.

I recall that night with the greatest clarity. As the two of us made our way home past the dimly burning gas lamps in the cool wet night, I was drunk for the first time in my life. It was not pretty, it was extremely distressing, and yet it had that something extra as well, a charm, a sweetness, it was insurrection and orgy, it was life and spirit. Beck bravely took an interest in me, although he bitterly reproached me as a bloody beginner, and he brought me, half-carried me home, where he succeeded in smuggling myself and himself through an open-standing corridor window.

With the disenchantment, however, to which I awoke after a quite short dead sleep with pain, an absurd woe came over me. I sat up in bed, still wearing my day-shirt, my clothes and shoes lay scattered on the floor and reeked of tobacco and vomit, and between headache, nausea, and a raging feeling of thirst an image came to mind which I had long since ceased to view. I saw home and parental house, father and mother, sisters and garden, I saw my quiet homey bedroom, saw the school and the marketplace, saw Demian and the Confirmation classes — and all this was light, all was in a blaze of splendor, all was wonderful, godly and pure, and all, all this had — so I knew now — still yesterday, still hours ago, belonged to me, waited for me and was now, first now in this hour, sunken and accursed, belonged to me no more, thrust me out, looked at me with disgust! All things dear and intimate, whatever I had experienced from my parents as far back as the most distant, most golden gardens of childhood, each kiss from my mother, each Christmas, each pious, bright Sunday morning at home, each flower in the garden — all of it was laid waste, all of it I had trampled underfoot! If the bailiff had come now and bound me and led me to the gallows as scum and temple-desecrator, I would have been in agreement, would have found it correct and good.

So this was how I looked on the inside! I, who went around and despised the world! I, who was proud in spirit and shared Demian's thoughts! This was how I looked, a piece of scum and a dirty pig, drunk and soiled, disgusting and common, a wild beast, taken unawares by horrible impulses! This was how I looked, I, who came out of those gardens, where all was purity, splendor, and sweet tenderness, I, who had loved the music of Bach and fine poetry! I heard still with disgust and indignation my own laughter, a drunken, unruly laughter breaking out jerkily and absurdly. That was I.

In spite of everything it was almost a pleasure to suffer these agonies. So long had I been blind and had crawled along insensibly, so long had my heart kept silent and sat impoverished in a corner, that even these self-accusations, this horror, this quite frightful feeling of the soul was welcome. It was still feeling, flames still rose, a heart was still beating therein! Confusedly I felt in the midst of misery something like liberation and springtime.

Meanwhile things went, seen from the outside, steadily downhill with me. The first drunken carouse was not the only one. There was much barhopping and monkey business in our school, I was one of the youngest among those who participated, and soon I was no longer one who had to borne with and a little boy, but rather a leader and star, a famous, neck-risking bar-frequenter. I belonged once again completely to the dark world, to the devil, and I passed in the world as a capital fellow.

At the same time it made me miserable. I lived from day to day in a self-destructive orgy, and while with my comrades I passed for a leader and a devil of a fellow, for a damned spirited and witty lad, I had an anguish-filled soul full of dread fluttering deep inside me. I still recall the tears coming to my eyes when upon leaving a bar on a Sunday morning I saw children playing in the street, bright and contented with freshly-combed hair and in their Sunday clothes. And while I, between beer laughs at the dirty tables of vulgar bars, entertained and often alarmed my friends through unheard-of cynicism, in my hidden heart I had reverence for everything that I derided and lay inwardly weeping on my knees before my soul, before my past, before my mother, before God.

That I never became one with my companions, that among them I remained lonesome and therefore could suffer so, that had a good reason. I was a barroom hero and scoffer after the hearts of the crudest, I showed spirit and showed courage in my thoughts and speech about teachers, school, parents, church — I could handle smut and perhaps dare to tell some myself — but I was never there when my comrades visited girls, I was alone and full of a glowing longing for love, hopeless longing, while according to my speech I ought to have been a seething sensualist. No one was more vulnerable, more bashful than I. And when I now and then saw the young city girls walking before me, pretty and clean, light and graceful, they were wonderful, pure dreams to me, a thousand times too good and pure for me. For a time I could not go anymore to Mrs. Jaggelt's stationery store because I blushed when I looked at her and thought about what Alphonse Beck had said concerning her.

The more I now was aware that in my new society too I would be perpetually lonely and different, the less I could get loose from it. I really don't know anymore whether the swilling and swaggering actually ever gave me pleasure, nor did I ever accustom myself to the drinking, so as not to experience painful consequences each time. It was all like a compulsion. I did what I had to do because otherwise I had no idea at all what to do with myself. I had a fear of being alone for long, a fear of the many tender, modest, heartfelt fits to which I was always inclined, a fear about the tender thoughts of love that came to me so often.

One thing I lacked the most — a friend. There were two or three fellow students whom I saw very willingly. But they belonged to the well-behaved, and my vices for the longest time were a secret to nobody! They avoided me. I was regarded by all as a hopeless player under whose feet the ground was slipping. The teachers were well-informed about me, I was severely punished many times, my final dismissal from the school was something expected. I myself knew this, for a long time now I was also not a good student anymore, but I pressed and swindled myself painstakingly through, with the feeling of not being able to endure it much longer.

There are many ways in which God can make us lonely and lead us to ourselves. This was the way He proceeded with me then. It was a bad dream. Over filth and stickiness, over broken beer glasses and cynical nights thoroughly chattered away I see myself, a spellbound dreamer, restless and tormented, crawling an ugly and unclean way. There are such dreams in which, on the way to the princess, one gets stuck in quagmires, in back-alleys full of stench and garbage. So it went with me. In this little refined fashion it was allotted me to become lonely and to bring between me and childhood a locked Eden-gate with pitilessly radiant guards. It was a beginning, an awakening of homesickness towards myself.

I still was terrified and had convulsions when for the first time, alarmed by letters from my schoolmaster, my father appeared in St. _____ and confronted me face to face. When he came, toward the end of the winter, for the second time, I was already hard and indifferent, let him chastise, let him entreat, let him call to mind my mother. He was in the end very angry and said if I didn't change he would let me be expelled with insult and infamy from the school and stick me in a reformatory. Let him! When he departed then, I felt sorry for him, but he had achieved nothing, he had found no way to me anymore, and there were moments when I felt it served him right.

What would become of me, that was all one to me. In my singular and not very pretty fashion, with my sitting in bars and crowing I was in conflict with the world, this was my form of protest. I made myself a wreck thereby and at times the matter appeared something like this: if the world could not use people like me, if it had no better place for them, no higher mission, well then people like me could just go kaput. Let the world suffer the loss.

The Christmas vacation that year was downright joyless. My mother was horrified when she saw me again. I had grown still more, and my haggard face looked gray and ravaged, with slack features and inflamed eye-rims. The first tinge of a moustache and the glasses which I had worn for a short time, made me even stranger to her. My sisters retreated and tittered. It was all unpleasant. Unpleasant and bitter the conversation with my father in his study, unpleasant the greeting with a few relatives, unpleasant above all the Christmas Eve. This had been, as long as I lived, the greatest day in our house, an evening of festivity and love, of gratitude, of the renewal of the bond between my parents and me. This time everything was only depressing and embarrassing. As usual my father read aloud the gospel story of the shepherds in the fields "keeping watch over their flocks there," as usual my sisters stood radiant before their table of gifts, but my father's voice sounded unjoyous, and my mother was sad, and to me it was all equally painful and unwished for, gifts and season's greetings, gospel story and tree of lights. The gingerbread smelled sweet and streamed forth thick clouds of sweeter memories. The Christmas tree exhaled a fragrance and told of things that were no more. I longed for an end to the evening and to the holidays.

It went on like this the entire winter. Only shortly before I had been forcibly warned by the teacher senate and threatened with expulsion. It could not last much longer. Well, for all I cared.

I had a particular grudge toward Max Demian. The whole time now I had no longer seen him. I had written him twice at the beginning of my school year in St. _____, but had received no answer; therefore I had also not visited him during the holidays.

In the same park where in the fall I had encountered Alphonse Beck, it happened in early spring, just as the thorn hedges begin to turn green, that I took notice of a girl. I was out for a walk by myself, full of loath-some thoughts and cares, for my health had become bad, and besides I was continually having money problems, owed sums to my comrades, had to invent necessary expenditures in order to again receive something from home, and had let the accounts for cigars and similar items increase in several stores. Not that these worries ran very deep — if sometime soon my being here took its end and I went into the water or was brought to the reformatory, then these few trifles didn't matter anymore either. But I lived nevertheless always face to face with such unlovely things and suffered under them.

On that spring day in the park I met a young lady that attracted me very much. She was tall and slender, elegantly dressed, and had an intel-ligent, boy's face. She pleased me immediately, she belonged to the type I loved, and she began to engage my fantasies. She was probably not much older than I, but much more finished, elegant and well-defined, almost a complete lady already, but with a tinge of wantonness and youthfulness in her face, which I liked exceedingly.

I had never succeeded in approaching a girl with whom I was in love, and I didn't succeed with this one either. But her impression was deeper than all the earlier ones, and the influence of this enamorment on my life was powerful.

Suddenly I had an image standing before me again, a lofty and reverent image — ah, and no need, no urge was so deep and vehement in me as the wish to respect and adore! I gave her the name Beatrice, for I knew about Beatrice, without having read Dante, from an English painting, a reproduction of which I had stored away. In it there was an English Pre-Raphaelite maidenly figure, very long-limbed and slender with a long, narrow head and etherealized hands and features. My fair young maiden did not quite match her, although she too showed this slenderness and boyishness of form that I loved, and something of the etherealness and soulfulness of face.

I never spoke a single word with Beatrice. Yet at that time she exerted the deepest influence upon me. She set her image up before me, she opened for me a sanctuary, she made me a worshipper in a temple. From one day to another I stayed away from the hard drinking and the nightly expeditions. I was able to be alone again, I loved to read again, I loved going for walks again.

The sudden conversion yielded me enough mockery. But I had now something to love and to adore, I had an ideal once more, life was once more full of presentiment and many-colored mystery-filled twilight — that made me unaffected. I was once more at home with myself, albeit only as the slave and servant of a revered image.

I cannot think of that time without a certain emotion. Again I tried with the innermost pains, from the fragments of a broken life-period to build myself a "light world," again I lived completely with the sole desire to do away with the dark and evil in me and abide fully in the light, on my knees before gods! All the same this present "light world" was somewhat my own creation; it was no longer a fleeing back and crawling under to mother and unanswerable safety, it was a new service, one invented and demanded by me myself, with responsibility and self-discipline. Sexuality, under which I suffered and before which I was always and ever in flight, was now to be transfigured into spirit and devotion by this sacred fire. It allowed for nothing gloomy anymore, nothing ugly, no groaning through the night, no heart palpitation before unchaste pictures, no eavesdropping at forbidden doors, no lasciviousness. Instead of all this I set up my altar, with the image of Beatrice, and in consecrating myself to her, I consecrated myself to the spirit and to the gods. That life-portion which I withdrew from the darker powers I sacrificed to the light. My goal was not joy, but purity, not happiness, but beauty and spirituality.

This cult of Beatrice changed my life completely. Yesterday still a precocious cynic, today I was a temple acolyte with the goal of becoming a saint. I not only renounced the bad life I had gotten accustomed to, I sought to change everything, sought to bring purity, nobility, and dignity to everything, thought hereon in eating and drinking, speech and attire. I began the morning with cold washings, to which I had a hard time forcing myself at first. I acted serious and dignified, carried myself upright and made my gait more slow and dignified. To onlookers it may have appeared comical — for me inside it was nothing but divine service.

Of all the new practices in which I sought expression for my new sentiment, one became important to me. I began to paint. It started with this, that the English Beatrice picture which I possessed was not enough like my girl. I wanted to try to paint her for myself. With a new joy and hope I carried into my room together — I had gotten one of my own a short while ago — beautiful paper, paints, and brushes, prepared palette, glass, porcelain dishes, pencils. The fine tempera colors in small tubes, which I had bought, delighted me. In with them there was a fiery chrome oxide green that I think I can still see today as it flashed up for the first time in the small, white dish.

I began with caution. Painting a face was difficult, I wanted to test it first elsewhere. I painted ornaments, flowers, and small imagined land-scapes, a tree by a chapel, a Roman bridge with cypresses. Sometimes I lost myself completely in these playful doings, was happy like a child with a coloring box. Finally, however, I began to paint Beatrice.

A few pages miscarried completely and were thrown away. The more I sought to place before me the face of the girl I had encountered now and then on the street, the less successful it would go. Finally I desisted from it and simply began to paint a face, following the imagination and the direction which came as a result of what was begun, out of the color and brush itself. It was a dreamed-up face that came forth thereby, and I was not dissatisfied with it. Yet I carried on the attempt at once, and each new page spoke somewhat more distinctly, came nearer the type, even though in no way the reality.

More and more I accustomed myself to it, to drawing lines with a dreaming paintbrush and filling in surfaces which were without a model, which resulted from playful touches, from the unconscious. At last, almost unconsciously, I finished a face that spoke more strongly to me than the earlier ones. It was not the face of that girl, it was never even supposed to be that for the longest time. It was something else, something unreal, but not any less precious. It looked more like a young man's head than the face of a girl, the hair was not light blonde as by my pretty girl, but brown with a reddish tinge, the chin was strong and solid, the mouth however, florid red, the whole somewhat stiff and mask-like but impressive and full of secret life.

As I sat in front of the finished painting, it made a strange impression upon me. It seemed to me a kind of divine image or holy mask, half-mascu-line, half-feminine, ageless, just as strong-willed as it was dreamy, just as rigid as it was secretly alive. This face had something to say to me, it belonged to me, it placed demands on me. And it bore a resemblance to someone, I didn't know with whom.

The portrait accompanied now for a while all my thoughts and shared my life. I kept it hidden in a drawer, so nobody could catch it and taunt me with it. But as soon as I was alone in my little room, I pulled the picture out and had relations with it. Evenings I fastened it with a pin to the tapestry across from over the bed, looked at it until I fell asleep, and mornings my first glance fell upon it.

It was precisely at this time that I again began to dream a lot, like I had always done as a child. It seemed to me as if I hadn't dreamed for years. Now they returned, a completely new set of images, and time after time the painted figure appeared therein, living and speaking, befriending me or hostile, sometimes distorted into a grimace and sometimes endlessly beautiful, harmonious, and noble.

And one morning, when I awoke from such dreams, I suddenly recognized it. It looked so fabulously familiar at me, it seemed to call my name. It seemed to know me like a mother, seemed turned toward me for all time. With palpitating heart I stared at the print, the brown, thick hair, the half-womanly mouth, the strong forehead with the singular brightness (it had dried up thus on its own), and nearer and nearer I felt in me the recognition, the rediscovery, the knowledge.

I sprang out of bed, drew myself up before the face, looked at it from the nearest nearness, directly into the wide-open, greenish, staring eyes, of which the right stood somewhat higher than the other. And all at once this right eye twitched, twitched lightly and finely, but clearly, and with this twitching I recognized the picture...

How could I have found it out only so late! It was Demian's face.

Later I compared the print over and over with Demian's actual features, as I found them in my memory. They were by no means the same, although similar. But it was Demian nevertheless.

Once on an early summer evening the sun shone slanting and red through my window which looked to the west. In the room it grew dusky. Then I came up with the idea of pinning the picture of Beatrice, or Demian, on the window crossbar and to gaze upon it as the evening sun shone through. The face dissolved without any outline, but the red-rimmed eyes, the brightness on the brow and the forceful red mouth glowed deep and wild from the level surface. Long I sat across from it, even after the light was already extinguished. And gradually a feeling came to me that this was not Beatrice or Demian, but — I myself. The picture didn't look like me — it wasn't supposed to either, I felt — but it was what determined my life, it was my inner self, my fate, or my daemon. So would my friend look, if I ever found one again. So would my beloved look, if I ever obtained one. So would my life and so would my death be, this was the sound and rhythm of my fate.

In those weeks I had begun some reading that made a deeper impression upon me than all that I had read before. Even later I have rarely experienced any book more so, except Nietzsche perhaps. It was a volume of Novalis, with letters and maxims of which many I did not understand and yet all of which unspeakably drew me in and surrounded me. One of his sayings struck me at the time. I wrote it with a pen under the portrait: "Fate and temperament are two names for one concept." That I now understood.

The girl that I named Beatrice I still encountered often. I felt no more agitation thereby, but always a gentle accord, a feeling-induced presentiment: you are linked with me, but not you, only your picture; you are a part of my destiny.

My yearning for Max Demian became powerful once more. I knew nothing of him, for years nothing. A single time I had met him during vacation. I see now that I have suppressed this brief meeting in my notes, and see that it happened out of shame and vanity. I must make up for it.

Thus once during vacation as I strolled with the blasé and always somewhat weary face of my tavern period through my native town, brandished my walking stick and looked at the philistines with their old, same as always, despised faces, there came up to me my erstwhile friend. Hardly had I seen him when I started all together. And lightning quick I couldn't help but think of Franz Kromer. How I wished Demian might have really forgotten this story! It was so unpleasant, having this obligation toward him — actually of course a silly children's story, but an obligation just the same...

He seemed to wait, to see whether I would greet him, and when I did as casually as possible, he gave me his hand. That was his handshake again! So firm, warm, and yet cool, manly!

He looked me attentively in the face and said: "You've grown tall, Sinclair." He himself seemed to me completely unchanged, equally old, equally young as always.

He joined me, we took a stroll and spoke about nothing but secondary things, nothing of former times. It occurred to me that I had written him more than once without getting a reply. Ah, let us hope he also forgot that, those stupid, stupid letters! He said nothing about them!

At that time there was still no Beatrice and no portrait, I was still in the middle of my time of dissolution. Outside of town I invited him to come with me into a tavern. He accompanied me. Ostentatiously I ordered a flask of wine, poured him some, clinked glasses with him and showed myself to be quite familiar with student drinking customs, emptying the first glass as well in one swallow.

"You go to taverns much?" he asked me.

"Oh, yes," I said lazily, "what else is there to do? In the end it's still what's most pleasurable."

"You think so? It may well be. Something about it is indeed very fine — the intoxication, the bacchantic! But I find that with most people who spend a lot of time sitting in bars that quality is completely lost. It seems to me there is something truly philistinish about this running to bars. Yes, one night long, with burning torches, to a true, fine drunkenness and reeling! But to do so again and again, one small glass after another, that is surely not the real thing, is it? Can you possibly imagine Faust sitting night after night on his barstool?"

I drank and shot him a hostile glance.

"Yes, it is certain that not everyone is a Faust," I said curtly.

He looked at me somewhat startled.

Then he laughed with the old freshness and superiority.

"Well, why fight over it? In any case the life of a drunkard or wastrel is presumably livelier than that of a blameless bourgeois. And then — I read this once — the life of a wastrel is one of the best preparations for being a mystic. It is indeed always such people as well like Saint Augustine that become visionaries. He too was formerly a pleasure-seeker and man of the world."

I was mistrustful and didn't want to let him be master over me in any way. So I said quite blasé: "Yes, each according to his own taste! As for me, speaking frankly, I want nothing whatsoever to do with becoming a visionary or something of that sort."

Demian darted a knowing look at me out of lightly pinched-in eyes.

"My dear Sinclair," he said slowly, "it was not my intention to say anything unpleasant to you. Besides — as to what end you now drink your pint, neither of us has any idea. That in you which makes up your life already knows it. It is so good to know this: that within us there is one who knows all, wills all, makes it all better than we ourselves. — But forgive me, I must go home."

Our leave-taking was brief. I remained sitting very discontented, completely finished the bottle, and found when I wanted to go that Demian had already paid the bill. This annoyed me even more.

By this small occurrence my thoughts now fastened onto Demian once more. They were full of Demian. And the words which he had said to me in that tavern outside of town came forth once more in my memory, strangely fresh and unlost. — "It is so good to know this, that within us there is one who knows all!"

I looked at the picture that hung on the window and was completely effaced. But I saw the eyes still glowing. That was the look of Demian. On it was the one who was inside me. The one who knows all.

What longing I had toward Demian! I knew nothing of him, he was out of my reach. I knew only that he was presumably a student somewhere and that after the close of his prep school time his mother had left our town.

As far back as my affair with Kromer I sought to retrieve all my memories of Max Demian. How much resonated there, what he had once said to me, and everything still made sense today, was actual, concerned me! Even that which he had said at our last, so little gratifying get-together about the wastrel and the saint stood suddenly clear before my soul. Wasn't that exactly how it had gone with me? Had I not lived in carouse and filth, stupefied and lost, until with a new life impulse precisely the opposite in me had come alive; the desire for purity, the longing for the holy?

So I went on with my recollections, it had long since grown dark and outside it was raining. Likewise in my memories I heard it raining, it was the hour under the chestnut trees, where he had once sounded me about Franz Kromer and divined my first secrets. One after another came forth, conversations on the way to school, Confirmation hours. And lastly, my first meeting of all with Max Demian occurred to me. And what was it all about then anyway? It didn't come to me immediately, but I gave myself time, I was completely immersed therein. And then it came back, even that. We were standing before my house, after he had imparted his opinion about Cain. Then he had spoken of the old, effaced coat of arms that sat above our house entrance, in the keystone which grew broader from bottom to top. He had said that it interested him, and that one must pay attention to such things.

In the night I dreamt of Demian and the coat of arms. It continually changed, Demian held it in his hands, often it was small and gray, often immensely large and many-hued, but he explained to me that it was still always one and the same. In the end, however, he obliged me to eat the coat of arms. When I had swallowed it, I sensed with tremendous terror that the engulfed heraldic bird was alive in me, beginning to fill me up and consume me from inside. Full of mortal terror I started up and awoke.

I became wide awake, it was the middle of the night, and I heard it raining into the room. I stood up to close the window and stepped thereby on something bright that lay on the floor. In the morning I found that it was my painted sheet. It lay in the wetness on the floor and had gotten warped into a roll. I stretched it to dry between blotting pages in a heavy book. When I looked at it again the next day, it was dry. It had changed however. The red mouth had grown pale and somewhat smaller. It was now altogether Demian's mouth.

I now set about painting a new picture, the heraldic bird. How it actually looked I no longer clearly knew, and some details about it were, as I knew, even from close up no longer well recognizable, since the thing was old and oftentimes painted over with color. The bird stood or perched on something, perhaps on a flower, or on a basket or a nest, or on a treetop. I didn't concern myself about it and began with that of which I had a clear idea. Out of an unclear need I began immediately with strong colors; the head of the bird was golden yellow on my sheet. Any time the mood struck me I did further work on it and completed the thing in several days.

Now it was a bird of prey, with a sharp, bold sparrow hawk's head. Half its body was stuck fast in a dark world globe, out of which it was working itself upwards as if out of a gigantic egg, upon a sky-blue background. The longer I considered it, the more and more it seemed to me to be like the colorful coat of arms as it had appeared in my dream.

To write a letter to Demian would not have been possible for me, even if I had known where to send it. I resolved, however, in that same dreamlike inkling-having with which I did everything at the time, to send him the picture with the sparrow hawk, whether it reached him or not. I wrote nothing on it, not even my name, carefully clipped the edges, bought a large paper envelope and wrote my friend's former address on it. Then I sent it off.

An exam was coming up, and I had to do more work than usual for school. The teachers had taken me into their favor once more, since I suddenly had changed my vile lifestyle. Even now I was certainly not a good student, but neither I nor anyone else still thought about the fact that a half year earlier my punitive dismissal from school had been entirely probable.

My father wrote me back again now in more of an earlier tone, without reproaches or threats. Still I had no inclination to explain to him or anyone else how the change in me had come about. It was an accident that this change corresponded with the wishes of my parents and teachers. This change did not bring me to the others, nor draw me nearer to anybody, it only made me lonelier. It was aimed somewhere, to Demian, to a distant fate. I did not know it myself, I was standing right in the middle of it. It had begun with Beatrice, but for some time I had been living with my painted sheets and my thoughts on Demian in such a totally unreal world that she too vanished completely from my eyes and thoughts. I could not have said a word to anyone about my dreams, my expectations, my inner transformation, not even if I had wanted to.

But how could I have wanted this?

CHAPTER FIVE. THE BIRD FIGHTS ITS WAY OUT OF THE EGG

My painted dream-bird was on its way and in search of my friend. In the strangest manner an answer came to me.

In my school class, on my desk, I once found, after the break between two lessons, a scrap of paper stuck in my book. It was folded exactly the same as was usual with us when school colleagues at times during a lesson would secretly pass notes to one another. I wondered only who had sent me such a note, for I stood in no such relation with any of my fellow students. I thought it would be an invitation to some schoolboy amusement, in which I would certainly take no part, and laid the scrap of paper unread in the front of my book. Only during the lesson did it chance to fall into my hands again.

I played with the paper, unfolded it thoughtlessly and found some words written on it. I threw a glance thereon, remained hanging on one word, became alarmed and read, while my heart contracted before fate as in great cold:

"The bird fights its way out of the egg. The egg is the world. He who wants to be born must destroy a world. The bird flies to God. That God's name is Abraxas."

I sank after the many readings of these lines into deep reflection: There was no possible doubt, it was an answer from Demian. No one could know

of the bird other than I or he. He had gotten my picture. He had understood and helped me interpret it. But how did all this hang together? And
— this plagued me above all — what did Abraxas mean? I had never heard
nor read the word. "The God's name is Abraxas!"

The hour passed, without my hearing anything of the instruction. The
next class began, the last of the morning; it was given by a young teacher's
assistant, who had only just come from the university and already pleased
us therefore, because he was so young and assumed no false airs towards
us.

We read under Doctor Follens' guidance Herodotus. This lecture
appertained to one of the few school subjects that interested me! But
this time I was somewhere else. I had opened the book mechanically, but
didn't follow the translation and remained sunk in my thoughts. Besides I
had already more than once come to experience how right that was, what
Demian had said to me at the time during our spiritual instruction. What
one wanted strongly enough, that succeeded. When I during instruction
was very strongly occupied with my own thoughts, then I could be at
peace, knowing the teacher would leave me in peace. Yes, when one was
absent-minded or sleepy, then he suddenly stood there: that too I had
already encountered. But when one was really thinking, really absorbed,
then one was protected. And I had also already tested this with a fixed
look and found it verified. During the times with Demian I did not succeed
with it, now I often sensed that one could accomplish very much with
looks and thoughts.

So I also sat now and was far from school. But then the voice of the
teacher struck unawares like lightning into my consciousness, so that I
awoke full of terror. I heard his voice, he stood close by me, I believed even
that he had called my name. I breathed a sigh of relief. Then I heard his
voice again. Loudly it said the word: "Abraxas."

In an explanation, whose beginning I had missed, Doctor Follens
continued: "We must not imagine the view of those sects and mystical
unions of antiquity to be as naïve as they appear from the standpoint of a
rationalistic consideration. Science in our sense was generally unknown
to antiquity. Instead there was a preoccupation with philosophical-
mystical truths, which were very highly developed. In part magic and
playful tricks arose from it, which probably often led as well to deceit and

crime. But the magic also had a noble origin and profound thoughts. As with the teaching of Abraxas, which I cited heretofore as an example. They mention this name in connection with Greek incantations and frequently deemed it the name of some magic demon, as some wild peoples even today still have. It seems, however, that Abraxas signifies much more. We can perhaps think of the name as that of a godhead which has the symbolic task of uniting the divine and the diabolical."

The small learned man went on speaking finely and eagerly, no one was very attentive, and when the name no longer came up, my attentiveness soon sank again back into myself.

"The divine and the diabolical uniting," it resounded in me. Here I could latch on. This was familiar to me from the conversations with Demian in the very latest time of our friendship. Demian had said then we perhaps had a god whom we could revere, but he only represented an arbitrarily separated half of the world (it was the official, sanctioned "light" world). One must be able to revere the whole world, however, thus one must either have a god who is also the devil or one must next to the divine service also arrange a service for the devil. — And now Abraxas was thus the god, who was as much God as devil.

For a time I sought out further with great zeal the trail without making any headway though. I even hunted throughout an entire library unsuccessfully for the Abraxas. But my nature was never strongly adapted to this kind of direct and conscious seeking, whereby one at first finds only truths which remain a stone in one's hand.

The figure of Beatrice with which I for a certain time was so much and so intimately occupied now gradually sank down, or rather it stepped slowly away from me, approaching the horizon more and more and becoming more shadowy, distant, and pallid. It satisfied the soul no more.

There now began to arise in my peculiar self-imprisoned existence, which I led like a sleepwalker, a new development. The longing for life bloomed in me, or rather the longing for love and the sex drive which I was able to dissolve for a while in the adoration of Beatrice, now demanded new images and objects. Still no fulfillment came to meet me, and it was more impossible than ever for me to deceive my longing and to expect something from the girls with whom my comrades sought their happiness. I had vivid dreams again, and to be sure more during the day than at night. Ideas, images, or wishes arose in me and drew me away from the outer world so that with these images inside me, with these dreams or shadows, I had truer and livelier relations and lived, than with my true surroundings.

A certain dream, or play of fancy, that always repeated itself, became meaningful to me. This dream, the most important and longest-lasting of my life, went something like this: I was returning to my father's house — above the doorway of the house shone the heraldic bird in yellow upon a blue background — in the house my mother came to meet me — but as I entered and was about to embrace her, it was not her but a never seen figure, large and powerful, resembling Max Demian and my painted print, but different, and in spite of its powerfulness utterly feminine. This figure drew me to itself and took me up in a deep, shuddering loving embrace. Rapture and terror were mingled together, the embrace was divine service just as much as it was a criminal offense. Too much remembrance of my mother, too much remembrance of my friend Demian haunted the figure which encompassed me. Its embrace gave offense to any reverence and was bliss nonetheless. Often I awoke from this dream with a profound feeling of happiness, often with deadly fear and a tortured conscience as from a terrible sin.

Only gradually and unconsciously did a union take place between this completely inner image and the hint that came to me from outside about the God to be sought there. Then, however, the union became closer and more intimate, and I began to sense that in this presentiment-dream I was directly invoking the Abraxas. Rapture and terror, man and woman mixed, the holiest and horriblest entangled in each other, deep guilt convulsing through tenderest innocence — such was my love-dream image, and such was Abraxas as well. Love was no longer the bestial dark drive such as I had felt with anguish in the beginning, and it was also no longer the pious spiritualized idolatry such as I had brought to the picture of Beatrice. It was both, both and yet much more, it was an angelic and Satanic figure, man and woman as one, human and animal, highest good and uttermost evil. To live this seemed to me determined, to make trial of this my destiny. I longed for it and was frightened of it, but it was always there, always above me.

In the following spring I was to leave the gymnasium and go on to study, I knew not where and what. On my lips grew a small beard, I was a full-grown man and yet completely helpless and without goals. Only one thing was certain: the voice inside me, the dream-image. I sensed the mission of blindly following this guidance. But it was difficult for me, and daily I rebelled. Perhaps I was mad, I thought not rarely, perhaps I was not like other men? But all that others performed I could also do, with a little diligence and effort I could read Plato, could solve trigonometric problems or follow a chemical analysis. Only one thing I couldn't do: tear out the dark hidden goal inside me and portray it there before me, as others did, who knew exactly what they wanted to be, professor or judge, doctor or artist, how long it would take and what kind of advantages it would provide. This I could not do. Perhaps I too would become something like that one day, but how was I to know? Perhaps I had to search and continue searching for years, and become nothing, and arrive at no goal. Perhaps I would even arrive at a goal, but it would be an evil, dangerous, terrible one.

I wanted nothing other than to try to live that which wanted to come out of me on its own. Why was that so very hard?

Often I made the attempt to paint the mighty love-formation of my dreams. I never succeeded. If I had succeeded, I would have sent the print to Demian. Where was he? I didn't know. I only knew that he was connected with me. When would I see him again?

The friendly repose of those weeks and months of the Beatrice era were long gone. At that time I thought I had reached an island and found some peace. But thus was it ever — hardly had a state become dear to me, hardly had a dream been pleasing to me when already it became withered and tarnished as well. In vain, to lament after it! I now lived in a fire of unappeased desire, of strained expectation that often made me completely wild and mad. The image of my dream-beloved I often saw before me with super-vivid distinctness, much more distinctly than my own hand, spoke with it, wept before it, cursed it. I called it mother and knelt before it in tears, I called it beloved and had a presentiment of its ripe, all-fulfilling kiss, I called it devil and whore, vampire and murderer. It enticed me away into the tenderest love-dreams and into dissolute shamelessness, nothing was too good and precious for it, nothing too bad and abject.

I passed that whole winter in an inner storm which I can hardly describe. I was long accustomed to the loneliness, it didn't oppress me; I lived with Demian, with the sparrow hawk, with the image of the dream figure which was my fate and my beloved. That was enough to live on, for everything expressed itself in vastness and open space, and every-thing pointed to Abraxas. But none of these dreams, none of my thoughts obeyed me, none could I call upon, not one could I give the colors I chose. They came and took me, I was ruled by them. I subsisted on them.

Well was I insured toward the outside world. I was not afraid of people, this even my fellow students had learned and evinced toward me a secret respect which often made me smile. If I wanted to I could see through most of them very well and amaze them on occasion thereby. Only I seldom or never wanted to. I was always occupied with myself, always with me myself. And I longed most ardently to finally also live a bit for once, to give something of myself to the world, to enter into relations and struggle with it. Sometimes in the evening when I ran through the streets and from unrest could not return home until midnight, sometimes I thought then, now and only now I must meet my beloved, passing by me on the nearest corner, calling me from the nearest window. Sometimes too this all seemed unbearably painful and I was prepared then to take my life once and for all.

A peculiar refuge I found then — by "accident" as they say. There are no such accidents however. If he who requires something necessary finds this necessary thing, then it is not the accident that gives him it, but he himself, his own longing for it and having to have it leads him there.

Two or three times on my walks through the town I had heard organ playing from a small suburban church without lingering there. When I came past the next time, I heard it again and recognized that it was Bach. I went to the gate, found that it was locked, and since the street was almost empty of people, I sat down next to the church on a curbstone, turned up my coat collar, and listened. It was not a large but a good organ, and it was strangely played, with a peculiar, highly personal expression of will and persistence that sounded like a prayer. I had this feeling: the man who plays here knows that a treasure is hidden in this music, and he woos and stamps his feet and takes pains for this treasure as for his life. I understand, in the technical sense, not very much about music, but from childhood on precisely this expression of the soul I have instinctively understood and have felt the musical as something self-evident in me.

The musician also played after that something modern, it could have been Reger. The church was almost completely dark, only a very thin gleam of light pierced through the nearest window. I waited until the music was over and then strolled back and forth until I saw the organist coming out. He was still a young man, but older than I, four-square and thick-set in figure, and he ran off quickly with powerful and as it were indignant strides.

From then on I often sat in the evening hour before the church or went back and forth. Once I even found the gate open and sat for half an hour shivering and happy in the pew while the organist above played by scanty gaslight. From the music that he played I heard not only him alone. It seemed to me that everything he played was related, that it had a secret coherence. Everything that he played was faithful, devoted, and pious, but not pious like the churchgoers and pastors, but pious like the pilgrims and beggars in the Middle Ages, pious with a thought-less devotion to a world-feeling that stands above all confessions. The masters before Bach were diligently played, and old Italians. And all said the same thing, all said that which the musician as well had in his soul: longing, innermost perception of the world and wildest sepa-rating of oneself again from it, ardent listening to one's own dark soul, the euphoria of surrender and profound curiosity about the miraculous. Once when I secretly followed him on his way out of the church, I saw him enter a small tavern far out on the edge of town. I couldn't resist and went in after him. For the first time I saw him here clearly. He sat at a table d'hôte in a corner of the small room, black felt hat on his head, a glass of wine before him, and his face was just as I expected it to be. It was ugly and somewhat wild, searching and obstinate, stubborn and self-willed, at the same time soft and child-like around the mouth. What was manly and strong sat all in the eyes and forehead, the lower part of the face was tender and unfinished, uncontrolled and feeble in part, the chin full of undecidedness stood there boyishly like a contradiction to his forehead and glance. His dark brown eyes, full of pride and hostility, those I liked.

Silently I sat down across from him, no one else was in the bar. He darted a glance at me, as if he wanted to chase me away. I held my ground however and looked at him unmoved until he morosely grumbled: "What are you looking at then so damned sharply? You want something from me?"

"I don't want anything from you," I said. "You've already given me much."

He knitted his brow.

"So, you're a music enthusiast? I find it loathsome to enthuse about music."

I didn't let myself be intimidated.

"I've listened to you quite often out there in the church," I said. "I don't want to bother you however. I thought perhaps I would find something by you, something special, I don't exactly know what. But better not to pay attention to me at all! I can certainly listen to you in the church."

"But I always lock up."

"Recently you forgot and I sat inside. Otherwise I stand outside or sit on the curbstone."

"Is that so? Next time you can come inside, it's warmer. You only have to knock on the door. But strongly, and not while I'm playing. Now fire away — what did you want to say? You're a very young man, probably a schoolboy or a college student. Are you a musician?"

"No. I like to listen to music, but only such as you play, quite unconditional music, such by which one senses that here a man is shaking heaven and hell. Music means so much to me, I believe, because it has so little morality. Everything else is moral, and I'm seeking something that isn't. I have always merely suffered on account of morality. I can't express myself well. — Do you know that there has to be a god who is both God and devil at the same time? There is supposed to have been one, I've heard of it."

The musician pushed his wide hat back and shook the dark hair from his large forehead. With that he looked at me penetratingly and inclined his face toward me across the table.

Softly and intently he asked: "What is the name of the god of whom you spoke there?"

"Unfortunately I know almost nothing about him, actually only his name. He is called Abraxas."

The musician looked with suspicion around him, as if someone could be listening in on us. Then he moved close to me and said in a whisper: "I thought so. Who are you?"

"I'm a grammar school student."

"Where do you know Abraxas from?"

"By accident."

He raised up the table so that his wine glass ran over.

"Accident! Don't talk any shit, young man! One does not know of Abraxas by accident, bear that in mind. I will tell you still more about him. I know a little bit concerning him."

He fell silent and moved his chair back. As I looked at him full of expectation, he made a wry face.

"Not here. Another time. — There, take some!"

With that he reached into the pocket of his coat, which he hadn't taken off, and drew out a pair of roasted chestnuts, which he threw toward me.

I said nothing, took and ate them and was very content.

"So!" he whispered after a while. "How do you know of — him?"

"I was alone and perplexed," I explained. "Then I remembered a friend from earlier years whom I believed knew very much. I had painted something, a bird, that was coming out from a globe. This I sent to him. After some time, when I no longer really thought about it, I received a piece of paper in my hand, on it stood this: 'The bird fights its way out of the egg. The egg is the world. He who wants to be born must destroy a world. The bird flies to God. The God's name is Abraxas'."

He said nothing in reply; we shelled our chestnuts and ate them with the wine.

"Should we order another bottle?" he asked.

"No, thanks. I don't like to drink."

He laughed, somewhat disappointed.

"As you wish! With me it's different. I'll stay here awhile. But you go now!"

When I went with him the next time then, after the organ music, he was not very communicative. He led me down an old alley and through an old, stately house up into a large, somewhat gloomy and neglected room, where outside of a piano nothing pointed to music, while a large bookcase and writing desk gave the room a somewhat scholarly feel.

"How many books you have!" I said appreciatively.

"A part of them is from the library of my father, with whom I live. — Yes, young man, I live with my father and mother, but I cannot introduce you to them, my acquaintances enjoy no great esteem here in this house. I am a prodigal son, you know. My father is a fabulously praiseworthy man, an important pastor and preacher in this town. And I, in order that you immediately know how things stand, am his gifted and very promising son, who, however, has gone off the rails and is to some degree mad. I was a divinity student and abandoned this trustworthy faculty shortly before my state exams. Although I'm still a specialist in it, as far as my private studies are concerned. What kinds of gods people at times have devised for themselves, that is to me still highly important and interesting. In other respects, I am presently a musician and will, it appears, soon obtain a little organist position. Then I'll be back with the church again, won't I?"

Along the spines of the books I looked, finding Greek, Latin, and Hebrew titles, so far as I could see by the weak light of the small table lamp. Meanwhile my acquaintance had lain down in the darkness by the wall on the floor and was busy with something there.

"Come," he called after a while, "now we will practice a little philos-ophy, that means shutting your mouth, lying on your belly, and thinking."

He struck a match and lit paper and logs in the fireplace, before which he lay. The flames rose high, he stirred and fed the fire with special care. I lay down beside him on the tattered carpet. He stared into the fire, which drew me in as well, and for an hour perhaps keeping silent we lay on our bellies before the flickering wood fire, saw it flaming and raging, sinking in and crumpling itself, flickering away and quivering and finally brooding in a quiet, sunken glow on the ground.

"Fire worship was not the stupidest thing ever invented," he muttered to himself at one time. Otherwise neither of us said a word. With staring eyes I was fixed on the fire, lost myself in dream and stillness, saw figures in the smoke and forms in the ashes. My comrade threw a small piece of resin into the glowing embers, a small, slender flame shot upwards, I saw in it the bird with the yellow sparrow hawk's head. In the fiery glow that was dying down, golden glowing threads ran together into nets, letters and forms appeared, memories of faces, of animals, of plants, of worms and serpents. As I, awakening, looked over at the other person, he was staring, his chin on his fists, devotedly and fanatically into the ashes.

"I must go now," I said softly.

"Yes, then go. Till we meet again!"

He didn't stand up, and since the lamp was extinguished, I had to grope my way with difficulty through the dark room and the dark passages and stairs out of the enchanted old house. On the street I halted and looked up at the old house. In no window was a light burning. A small brass plate gleamed in the luster of the gas lantern before the door.

"Pistorius, Pastor primarius," I read on it.

Only at home, when after supper I was sitting alone in my little room, did it occur to me that I had not learned anything else about Abraxas or Pistorius, that in general we had hardly exchanged ten words. But I was very pleased by my visit with him. And for next time he had promised me a quite exquisite piece of old organ music, a passacaglia by Buxtehude.

Without my knowing it, the organist Pistorius had given me my first lesson, when I was lying on the floor with him before the fire in his gloomy recluse room. The gazing into the fire had done me good, it had strengthened and confirmed inclinations in me which I had always had but never had actually cultivated. Gradually those things were in part becoming clear to me.

Even as a young boy I had now and then the propensity to contemplate bizarre forms in Nature, not observing but surrendering to their own individual magic, their intricate, profound language. Long, wood-decayed tree roots, colored veins in stone, spots of oil that swim upon the water, fissures in glass — all things like this possessed great magic for me at the time, above all as well fire and water, smoke, clouds, dust, and most especially the revolving flecks of color that I saw when I closed my eyes. In the days after my first visit with Pistorius this began to take hold of me once more. Then I noticed that a certain strengthening and joy, an enhancing of my feeling about myself, which I sensed since that time, was entirely thanks to the long staring into the fire. It was remarkably comforting and enriching to do this!

To the few experiences which I had found hitherto on the way to my actual life's goal this new one arranged itself: the viewing of such formations, the surrendering oneself to the irrational, irregular, strange forms of Nature engenders in us a feeling of the harmony of our inner self with the will which allows these formations to come to be — we soon sense the temptation to think of them, to take them for our own moods, for our own creations — we see the boundary between us and Nature trembling and dissolving and become acquainted with the state of mind in which we don't know whether the images on our retina stem from outer or inner impressions. Nowhere so simply and easily as by this exercise do we make the discovery how very much we are creators, how very much our souls continually partake in the perpetual creation of the world. Rather it is the same indivisible deity, which is active in us and in Nature, and if the outer world should go under, then one of us would be capable of building it up again, for mountain and stream, tree and leaf, root and blossom, everything formed in Nature lies pre-formed in us, stems from the soul, whose essence we do not know, which for the most part, however, gives us a sense of loving power and creative power.

Only many years later did I find this observation confirmed in a book, by Leonardo da Vinci, namely, who once speaks about how good and deeply stirring it is to look at a wall which is spit upon by many people. Before every stain on the moist wall he must have felt the same as Pistorius and I before the fire.

At our next get-together the organ player gave me an explanation.

"We always describe the boundaries of our personality too narrowly! We reckon to our person always merely that which we recognize as individually different, as diverging. We consist, however, of the whole consistency of the world, each one of us, and just as our bodies carry in themselves the genealogical table of development down to the fish and even farther back, so we have in our souls all that has ever lived in the souls of men. All the gods and devils that have ever been, be it by the Greeks and Chinese or by the Zulus, all are together in us, are there as possibilities, as wishes, as ways out. If mankind were to die out except for a single halfway gifted child who had enjoyed no instruction of any kind, then this child would rediscover the entire course of things, it would be capable of producing everything again, there would be gods, demons, paradises, Old and New Testaments."

"That's fine," I demurred, "but wherein does the value of the individual still exist then? Why do we go on striving if everything in us is already complete?"

"Halt!" cried Pistorius vehemently. "There is a big difference whether you merely carry the world in yourself or whether you also know it! A madman can bring forth thoughts reminiscent of Plato, and a little pious schoolboy in a Moravian institute creatively follows deep mythological connections proposed by the Gnostics or Zoroaster. But he knows nothing about them! He is a tree or a stone, an animal at best, as long as he does not know it. Then, however, when the first spark of this recognition dawns, then he becomes human. You would certainly not regard all the bipeds that run there on the street as human beings merely because they walk upright and carry their young for nine months, would you? Surely you see how many of them are fish or sheep, worms or leeches, how many ants, how many bees! Well, in each of them the possibilities of becoming human are there, but only by man having a presentiment of them, only by even partly learning to be made conscious of them do these possibilities then belong to him."

Our conversations were of this sort. They seldom brought me something completely new, something utterly surprising. All, however, even the most banal, struck with a soft constant hammer blow on the same point in me, all helped me shed layers of skin, shatter eggshells, and from each I raised my head somewhat higher, somewhat freer, until my yellow bird pushed his fair raptor's head out of the demolished world shell.

Frequently we also related our dreams to each other. Pistorius knew how to interpret them. A singular example I remember just now. I had a dream in which I could fly, in such a way, however, that I in a certain measure was slung by a large swing through the air, whose master I was not. The feeling of this flight was elevating, but soon turned to fear, when I saw myself dragged to suspicious heights with no will of my own. Then I made the redeeming discovery that I could regulate my rising and falling through the holding and releasing of my breath.

To which Pistorius said: "The swing that makes you fly is our great human possession, which each one has. It is the feeling of connection with the roots of every force, but it soon makes one anxious therewith! It is damned dangerous! That is why most people desist from flying and prefer to walk with the aid of fixed rules on the civic pathway. But not you. You continue flying, as if it were suitable for an able young men. And behold, there you discover the strange thing, that you gradually become master over it, that in addition to the great general force that sweeps you away there comes a subtle, small, special force of your own, an organ, a helm. That is splendid! Without that one would go with no will of one's own into the air, that, for example, is what madmen do. Deeper presentiments are given to them than to the people on the civic pathway, but they have no key and no helm as well and whiz off into the bottomless deep. But you, Sinclair, you make it work! And how, please? That you still don't know at all, do you? You do it with a new organ, with a breath regulator. And now you can see how little of the 'personal' your soul possesses in its depths. Namely, it doesn't invent this regulator! It is not new! It is a loan, it has existed for thousands of years. It is the equilibrium organ of fish, the swim bladder. And in fact there are a few strange and conservative species of fish even today in which the swim bladder is a kind of lung and at the same time can rightly serve for breathing under certain circumstances. Thus exactly down to a hair like the lung which you in your dream use as a flying bladder!"

He even brought me a volume of zoology and showed me names and illustrations of these outmoded fish. And I felt in me, with a peculiar shudder, a function from an earlier evolutionary epoch alive in me.

Chapter Six. Jacob's Struggle

What I came to know about Abraxas from the singular musician Pistorius I cannot briefly recount. The most important thing, however, that I learned from him was a further step on the way to myself. I was at the time, with my eighteen years or so, an unusual young man, in a hundred things precocious, in a hundred other things very backward and helpless. When I compared myself with others now and again, I was often proud and conceited, but just as often depressed and humiliated. Often I took myself for a genius, often for half-mad. I did not succeed in taking part in the joys and lives of my contemporaries, and often I was consumed in reproaches and worries, as though I was hopelessly separated from them, as though life was closed to me.

Pistorius, who was himself a full-grown original, taught me to maintain my courage and self-respect. While in my words, in my dreams, in my fantasies and thoughts he always found something valuable, always took them seriously and discussed them in earnest, he set an example for me.

"You told me," he said, "that you love music because it is not moral. Fair enough. But you yourself must also not be a moralist then! You are not allowed to compare yourself with others, and if Nature has made you a bat you are not allowed to make yourself into an ostrich. You sometimes think of yourself as odd, you reproach yourself for going a different way than most others. This you must unlearn. Look into the fire, look into the clouds, and as soon as the presentiment comes and the voices in your soul begin to speak, then give yourself up to them and don't ask first whether perhaps it might also pass or be pleasing to your teacher or your father or some dear god or other! With that one ruins oneself. With that one arrives at the civic pathway and become a fossil. Dear Sinclair, the name of our god is Abraxas, and he is God and Satan, he has the light and the dark world in himself. Abraxas has no objection to any of your thoughts or any of your dreams. Never forget that. But he will forsake you once you become blameless and normal. Then he will forsake you and seek another pot wherein to cook his thoughts."

Among all my dreams that dark love-dream was the truest. Often, often have I dreamed it, stepped aside underneath the heraldic bird in our old house, wanted to draw my mother to me and held instead of her in my arms the large, half-manly, half-motherly woman, of whom I was afraid and yet to whom I was drawn with the most ardent longing. And this dream I could never relate to my friend. I kept it back when I had disclosed all the others to him. It was my corner, my secret, my refuge.

When I was distressed, then I asked Pistorius if he might play old Buxtehude's passacaglia. In the dark, evening church I sat then lost in this strange, intimate, submerged-in-itself, self-eavesdropping music, which did me good and made me more prepared to acknowledge the right of the voices in my soul.

At times we remained a while, even after the organ had already faded away, sitting in the church and seeing the weak light shine through the high, pointy-arched windows and lose itself.

"It sounds comical," said Pistorius, "that I was once a theology student and almost became a parson. But it was only an error in the form that I committed thereby. To be a priest is my calling and my goal. Only I was satisfied too early and placed myself at the disposal of Jehovah before I even knew about Abraxas. Ah, every religion is beautiful. Religion is soul, it is immaterial whether one partakes of Christian Communion or goes on a pilgrimage to Mecca."

"Then you could, however," I suggested, "still actually become a parson."

"No, Sinclair, no. I would be obliged to lie. Our religion is practiced as if it were not one. It is carried out as if it were an intellectual exercise. A Catholic I could well be out of necessity, but a Protestant priest — no! The few actual believers — I know such people — adhere with pleasure to the literal, to them I could not say, for example, that for me Christ is not a person but a hero, a myth, an enormous shadow-image in which mankind can see itself painted on the wall of eternity. And the others, those who come to Church to hear a clever word, to fulfill a duty, to neglect nothing and so on, why, what could I have to say to them? Convert them, you think? But I have no wish to do that at all. The priest doesn't want to convert, he wants to live only among believers, among his like, and he wants to be the bearer and expression for the feeling from which we make our gods."

He broke off. Then he continued: "Our new faith, for which we now choose the name of Abraxas, is beautiful, my dear friend. It is the best we have. But it is still a fledgling! Its wings are not yet grown. Alas, a lonesome religion, that is not yet the true one. It must be combined some, it must have cult and rapture, feasts and mysteries..."

He mused and became lost in himself.

"Can't one also celebrate mysteries alone or in the smallest circle?" I asked hesitantly.

"One can indeed," he nodded. "I've been celebrating them for quite a while. I have celebrated cults for which I would have had to sit away for years in prison, if people had known about them. But I know it is still not the right thing."

Suddenly he clapped me on the shoulder so that I started all together. "Boy," he said affectingly, "you have mysteries as well. I know that you must have dreams that you don't tell me. I don't want to know them. But I say to you: live them, live these dreams, play them out, build altars to them! It is not yet the absolute, but it is a route. Whether we will someday, you and I and a few others, come to renew the world, that will be seen. But within us we must renew it every day, otherwise it is nothing to us. Think on that! You are eighteen years old, Sinclair, you don't go running to street hussies, you must have love dreams, love wishes. Perhaps you are such as to be afraid of them. They are the best thing you have! You can believe me. I lost a lot therewith at your age. I did violence to my love dreams. One must not do this. When one knows of Abraxas, one is not allowed to do this anymore. One is allowed to fear nothing and to look upon nothing that the soul desires in us as forbidden."

Startled, I objected: "But one cannot just do whatever enters one's head! One also cannot just kill a man because one finds him repugnant."

He moved closer to me.

"Under certain circumstances even that is allowed. Only most of the time it is a mistake. And I don't mean you should simply do everything that strikes your fancy. No, but you shouldn't do these sudden ideas, which make good sense, harm by driving them away and moralizing about them. Instead of nailing oneself or another to the Cross, one can drink wine from a chalice together with celebratory thoughts and thereby think on the mystery of the sacrifice. One can, even without such handlings, handle one's drives and so-called temptations with love and respect. Then they will show you their sense, and they all make sense. — If something downright nonsensical or sinful occurs to you again, Sinclair, if you want to kill somebody or commit some gigantic act of nastiness, then think for a moment that it is Abraxas fantasizing thus in you! The man whom you would like to kill is indeed never Mister So-and-so, he is surely only a disguise. If we hate a man, then we hate in his figure something which sits in ourselves. What does not exist in ourselves, that does not engage us."

Never had Pistorius said something that struck so deeply into my most secret. I could not respond. But what had affected me most strongly and singularly was the consonance of this exhortation with the words of Demian, which I had borne in me for years and years. They knew nothing of each other, and both had said the same thing to me."

"The things which we see," said Pistorius softly, "are the same things which are in us. There is no reality other than the one which we have in us. That is why most men live such unreal lives, because they take the outside images for real and do not allow their own world inside themselves any chance to speak at all. Thereby one can be happy. But once one knows the other, then one no longer has the choice of going the way of most people. Sinclair, the way of most people is easy, ours is hard. — Let us go."

Some days later, after I had waited twice in vain for him, I met him late at night on the street, as he came alone around a corner, blown in the cold night wind, stumbling and completely drunk. I had no mind to call to him.

He came past, without seeing me, and stared before himself with glowing and lonely eyes, as if he were following a dark call from the unknown. I followed him the length of a street, he drifted along as though pulled by an invisible thread, with a fanatical and yet relaxed gait, like a ghost. Sadly I went back home to my unfulfilled dreams.

"Thus he now renews the world in himself!" I thought and yet felt in the same moment that it was low and moralistic in thinking. What did I know of his dreams? Perhaps in his intoxication he went the more certain way than I in my anxiety.

In the pauses between school periods it had occurred to me at times that a fellow student sought my company, one to whom I had never paid any attention. He was a small, weak-looking, slender youth with reddish-blond thin hair, who in look and behavior had something all his own. One evening, when I was coming home, he was lurking for me in the alley, let me pass by him, then ran after me again and stood by our front door.

"Do you want something from me?" I asked.

"I would simply like to speak with you once," he said shyly. "Be so good and walk a few steps with me."

I followed him and sensed that he was deeply agitated and full of expectation. His hands trembled.

"Are you a spiritualist?" he asked quite suddenly.

"No, Knauer," I said laughing. "Not a trace of it. How did you come up with such a thing?"

"But you are a theosophist?"

"Not that either."

"Ah, don't be so secretive! I sense quite well indeed that there is something special about you. One can see it in your eyes. I believe for certain that you have communication with spirits. — I don't ask out of curiosity, Sinclair, no! I am myself a seeker, you know, and I am so alone."

"Just explain!" I urged him on. "I know absolutely nothing at all about spirits, I live in my dreams and that is what you have sensed. Other people also live in dreams, but not in their own, that is the difference."

"Yes, perhaps that is so," he whispered. "It's only a question of what kind of dreams they are in which one lives. — Have you ever heard of white magic?"

I had to deny it.

"It is when one learns to be master of oneself. One can become immortal and cast spells as well. Have you ever engaged in such practices?"

Upon my inquisitive question about these practices he acted mysterious at first, until I turned to go, then he opened up.

"For instance, when I want to fall asleep or likewise want to concentrate, then I engage in such a practice. I think about something, for instance a word or a name, or a geometric figure. I then think it into myself, as strongly as I can, I seek to imagine it inside my head, until I feel it is in there. Then I think it in the throat, and so on, until I am completely filled by it. Then I am quite steadfast, and nothing can disturb me anymore."

I grasped to a certain degree what he meant. Yet I felt sure that he had something else at heart, he was strangely agitated and hasty. I sought to make his asking easy, and soon he came forth with his actual concern.

"You are continent too, aren't you?" he asked me anxiously.

"How do you mean that? Do you mean sexually?"

"Yes, yes. I have been continent for two years now, ever since I was aware of the doctrine. Previously I practiced vice, you know what I mean. So you have never been with a woman?"

"No," I said. "I have never found the right one."

"But if you were to find one whom you thought was the right one, then you would sleep with her?"

"Yes, naturally. — If she had nothing against it," I said somewhat mockingly.

"Oh, there you're on the wrong road though! One's inner powers can only be improved when one remains completely continent! I've been at it for two years, two years and something more than a month! It is so difficult! Sometimes I can barely hold out anymore."

"Listen, Knauer, I don't believe that continence is so terribly important."

"I know," he said defensively, "they all say that. But I didn't expect it from you. He who wants to take the higher spiritual path must remain pure, unconditionally!"

"Well, then do it! But I don't understand why one who suppresses his sexuality should be 'purer' than anyone else. Or can you eliminate sexuality from all your thoughts and dreams too?"

He looked at me despairingly.

"No, certainly not! Good Lord, and yet it must be. I have dreams in the night that I couldn't even tell to myself. Terrible dreams, you!"

I was reminded of what Pistorius had said to me. But as much as I felt his words to be right, I could not pass them on, I could not impart advice which was not derived from my own experience and whose observance I myself did not yet feel equal to. I grew silent and felt myself humiliated in that here somebody sought advice from me and I had none to give him.

"I've tried everything!" yammered Knauer by my side. "I've done what one can do, with cold water, with snow, with gymnastics and running, but none of it helps. Each night I awake from dreams on which I dare not think at all. And the horrible thing is because of it everything is gradually getting lost again by me that I learned spiritually. I can hardly bring it off anymore, getting myself to concentrate or to fall asleep, often I lie awake the whole night. I can't hold out much longer. If finally though I can't get through the struggle, if I give up and make myself unclean again, then I'll be worse than all the others who never have struggled at all. You understand that, don't you?"

I nodded but could say nothing in response. He began to bore me, and I was startled at myself that his openly visible distress and despair made no deeper impression on me. I only felt: I cannot help you.

"So you have nothing at all for me?" he finally said, exhausted and sad. "Nothing at all? There must be a way though! How do you do it then?"

"I can't tell you anything, Knauer. People can't help each other there. Nobody helped me, either. You must reflect upon yourself, and then you must do that which actually comes from your being. There is no other way. If you can't find yourself, then you won't find any spirits either, I believe."

Disillusioned and suddenly grown dumb, the little fellow looked at me. Then a sudden hatefulness glowed up in his glance, he made a wry face at me and cried angrily: "Ah, a fine saint you are! You have your vices too, I know it! You act like a wise man and are secretly attached to the same filth as me and everyone else! You're a swine, a swine; like I myself! We're all swine!"

I went away and left him standing there. He did like me for two or three steps, then he remained behind, turned around, and ran off. I felt ill from a feeling of pity and disgust, and I did not get free of the feeling until at home in my small little room I set my few pictures around me and gave myself up to my own dreams with the most ardent sincerity. Then at once my dream came again, the dream of the doorway and the coat of arms, of the mother and the strange woman, and I saw the features of the woman so super-clearly that even that same evening I began to draw her picture.

When this drawing was finished after several days, spread out in dream-like quarter-hours as though unconsciously, I hung it up in the evening on the wall, moved the study lamp in front of it and stood before it as before a ghost, with which I had to struggle until a decision was reached. It was a face similar to the earlier one, similar to my friend Demian, in some features also similar to me myself. One eye stood strikingly higher than the other, the gaze went above me away in sunken glassiness, full of fate.

I stood before it and became cold right down into the breast because of the inner exertion. I questioned the picture, I accused it, I caressed it, I prayed to it; I called it mother, called it beloved, called it whore and hussy, called it Abraxas. In between words from Pistorius — or from Demian? — occurred to me; I couldn't remember when they were spoken, but I thought I heard them again. They were words about Jacob's struggle with the angel of God and his "I will not let thee go except thou bless me."

The painted face in the lamplight changed with each invocation. It became bright and shining, became black and gloomy, closed faded lids over died-away eyes, opened them again and flashed glowing looks, it was woman, it was man, it was girl, it was a small child, an animal, it dissolved into a speck, became large and clear once more. In the end, following a strong, inner summons, I closed my eyes and saw now the picture inside of me, stronger and more powerful. I wanted to kneel down before it, but it was so much a part of me that I could not separate it from myself anymore, as if it had become nothing but ego.

Then I heard a dark, heavy roaring as from an early spring storm and trembled with an indescribable new feeling of anxiety and experience. Stars started convulsively before me and were extinguished, memories going back to the first, most forgotten period of childhood, back indeed to pre-existence and early stages of development, streamed crowdedly on past me. But the memories, which seemed to repeat my whole life down into what was most secret, did not cease with yesterday and today, they went farther, mirroring the future, tearing me away from today and into new forms of life whose images were tremendously clear and blinding, not one of which I could correctly remember later however.

In the night I awoke out of a deep sleep, I was clothed and lay cross-wise on the bed. I lit a candle, felt that I had to recollect something important, knew nothing more of the hours before. I lit a candle, the recollection came gradually. I searched for the picture, it no longer hung on the wall, lay not on the table either. Then I thought I dimly recalled that I had burned it. Or was this a dream, that I had burned it up in my hands and eaten the ashes?

A great convulsive unrest drove me. I put on my hat, went through house and lane as though under compulsion, ran and ran through streets and across squares as though blown along by a storm, lay in wait before the gloomy church of my friend, searched and searched in dark urge, without knowing for what. I came through a suburb, where whorehouses stood, there was still light here and there. Further outside lay newly built structures and heaps of bricks, partially covered with gray snow. It entered my head, as I drifted like a dream-walker under a strange impulse through these deserts, the new building in my native town, the one into which my tormentor at our first settling of accounts had once dragged me. A similar building lay here before me in the gray night, yawning at me with its black entryway. It drew me in, I wanted to avoid it and stumbled over sand and rubble; the impulse was stronger, I had to go in.

Across boards and broken bricks I staggered into the desolate space, it smelled drearily of moist coldness and stone. A sandheap lay there, a light gray spot, everything else was dark.

Then a terrified voice called to me: "For God's sake, Sinclair, where did you come from?"

And next to me out of the darkness a human being rose up, a little meager lad, like a ghost, and I recognized even while my hair stood on end my school comrade Knauer.

"How did you come here?" he asked, as if delirious with excitement. "How were you able to find me?"

I did not understand.

"I was not looking for you," I said, benumbed; every word pained me and came to me painstakingly via dead, heavy, as if frozen lips.

He stared at me.

"Weren't looking?"

"No. I was drawn here. Did you call me? You must have called me. What are you doing here then? It's night after all."

He embraced me convulsively with his thin arms.

"Yes, night. Soon it will be morning. O Sinclair, you haven't forgotten me! Can you forgive me then?"

"What then?"

"Alas, I was so odious!"

Only now did the memory of our conversation come to me. Was that four, five days ago? It seemed to me a lifetime had gone by since then. But now I suddenly knew everything. Not only what had happened between us, but also why I had come here and what Knauer had wanted to do outside here.

"So you wanted to take your life, Knauer?"

He shuddered with cold and with fear.

"Yes, I wanted to. I don't know whether I would have been able to. I wanted to wait until morning."

I dragged him out into the open. The first horizontal light-streaks of day glimmered unspeakably cold and joyless in the gray atmosphere.

I led the boy by the arm a stretch further. Out of me there spoke: "Now you go home and don't say a thing to anyone! You went down the wrong path, the wrong path! We aren't swine either, as you think. We are men. We make gods and struggle with them, and they bless us."

Silently we walked further and asunder. When I returned home, it was already break of day.

The best that I still brought away from that time in St. _____ were hours with Pistorius at the organ or before his fireplace. We read a Greek text about Abraxas together, he read aloud to me pieces of a translation from the Vedas and taught me to pronounce the sacred "Om." Nevertheless it was not these learned things which furthered me in my inner self, but rather the opposite. What benefited me was the advancing discovery in my self, the increasing trust in my own dreams, thoughts and presentiments, and the increasing knowledge of the power that I carried within me.

Pistorius and I understood one another in every way. I needed only to think strongly on him, then I was certain that he or a greeting from him would come to me. I could ask him anything, just as with Demian, without his even being there: I needed only to solidly place him before me and direct my questions at him as intensive thoughts. Then all the psychic power given in the question came back as answer in me. Only it wasn't the person of Pistorius, nor that of Max Demian, that I placed before me, but the image dreamed up and painted by me, the man/womanly dream image of my daemon that I had to invoke. No longer did it live only in my dreams and no longer only on paper, but inside me, as an ideal and an intensification of myself.

It was peculiar and at times comical, the relationship into which the failed suicide Knauer had entered with me. Since the night in which I had been sent to him, he was attached to me like a faithful servant or dog, sought to join his life with mine, and followed me blindly. He came to me with the strangest questions and wishes, wanted to see ghosts, wanted to learn the Cabala, and didn't believe me when I assured him that I understood nothing of all these matters. He thought there was no power I didn't possess. But the odd thing was that he often came to me with his strange and stupid questions precisely when I had some knot to undo, and that his whimsical ideas and requests often brought me the key word and the impulse toward a solution. Often he was a nuisance to me and would be sent away imperiously, but yet I sensed: he too had been sent to me, from him too came back that which I had given him, doubled back in me, he too was a leader to me, or at least a way. The absurd books and writings that he brought to me and in which he sought his salvation taught me more than I could perceive at that moment.

This Knauer later disappeared from my way unfelt. With him an explanation was not necessary. But with Pistorius to be sure. With this friend I still experienced toward the end of my school time in St. _____ something peculiar.

Even harmless people are hardly spared once or several times in life from coming into conflict with the fine virtues of piety and gratitude. Each one of us must at some time take the step that separates him from his father, from his teachers, each must experience something of the hardness of loneliness, even if most people can endure little of it and soon crawl under once more. — From my parents and their world, the "light" world of my fair childhood, I was not divided by a violent struggle but slowly and almost imperceptibly came to be more distant and estranged. I felt sorry, it often made for bitter hours during my visits home; but it didn't penetrate to the heart, it was tolerable.

But there where we have offered not out of habit but out of our most specially own impulse of love and respect, there where we with our most specially own hearts have been disciples and friends — there it is a bitter and terrible moment, when we suddenly come to realize that the leading current in us wants to lead us away from our loved one. Then every thought that rejects the friend and teacher directs itself with a poisonous spine towards our own heart, every defensive blow strikes one's own face. Then emerges, in him who meant to bear a valid morality in himself, the names "perfidy" and "ingratitude" like catcalls and stigmas, then the frightened heart flees back fearfully into the dear valleys of childhood virtues and cannot believe that this break too must be made, that this bond too must be cut to pieces.

With time a feeling inside me had slowly turned against recognizing my friend so unconditionally as a leader. What I had experienced in the most important months of my adolescence was the friendship with him, his advice, his solace, his nearness. Out of him God had spoken to me. Out of his mouth my dreams had returned to me, clarified and interpreted. He had given me faith in myself. — Ah, and now I sensed a slowly growing resistance toward him. I heard too much didacticism in his words, I felt that only a part of me he completely understood.

There was no conflict, no scene between us, no break and not even a settling of accounts. I said to him only a single, actually harmless word — but it was yet precisely the moment in which between us an illusion disintegrated into colorful fragments.

An inkling beforehand had already oppressed me for a while, becoming a distinct feeling one Sunday in his old study. We lay on the floor before the fire, and he spoke of mysteries and forms of religion, which he studied, on which he reflected, with whose possible future he was occupied. To me, however, this all seemed more curious and interesting than vitally important, it sounded like erudition to me, it sounded to me like a weary searching among the ruins of former worlds. And all at once I felt a repugnance toward this whole method, toward this cult of mythologies, toward this mosaic-game with handed-down forms of belief.

"Pistorius," I suddenly said, with a malice breaking forth that was surprising and frightening to me myself, "you ought to tell me a dream again sometime, an actual dream that you've had in the night. This, what you speak here, is so — so damned antiquarian!" He had never heard me speak in this manner, and I myself at the same moment felt lightning-quick with shame and horror that the arrow, which I had shot at him and which had struck him in the heart, had come from his own arsenal — that I was now throwing maliciously toward him in pointed form self-reproaches which I had occasionally heard him express in an ironical tone.

He sensed it instantly, and he fell silent immediately. I looked at him with anguish in my heart and saw him turn frightfully pale.

After a long pregnant pause he placed a fresh log on the fire and quietly said: "You're quite right, Sinclair, you're a clever fellow. I'll spare you the antiquarian stuff."

He spoke very calmly, but well I heard the pain of the wounding come out. What had I done?

I was close to tears, I wanted to be cordial toward him, wanted to ask his forgiveness, wanted to assure him of my love, of my tender gratitude. Stirring words occurred to me — but I could not say them. I remained lying there, gazed into the fire, and was silent. And he too was silent, and so there we lay, and the fire burned and sank down, and with each fading-to-pale flame I felt something beautiful and intimate dying away and fleeing away, which could never come back again.

"I'm afraid you've misunderstood me," I said finally, very choked-up and with a dry, hoarse voice. The stupid, senseless words came over my lips as if mechanically, as if I were reading aloud from a newspaper novel.

"I understand you all right," said Pistorius softly. "You're certainly right." He waited. Then he went on slowly: "In just so far as one man can be right toward another."

No, no, a voice cried out in me, I'm wrong! — but I could say nothing. I knew that with my single, little word I had alluded to an essential weakness, to his need and wound. I had touched the point where he was bound to mistrust himself. His ideal was "antiquarian," he was a backwards seeker, he was a Romantic. And suddenly I felt deeply: precisely that, which Pistorius had been to me and had given to me, that he could not be and give to himself. He had led me on a path that had to step over and leave even him, the leader, behind.

God knows how such a word arises! I had not meant it badly at all, had had no presentiment of a catastrophe. I had spoken out about something which in the moment of speaking out itself I was thoroughly unaware of, I had yielded to a small, somewhat witty, somewhat malicious conceit, and it turned out to be fate. I had committed a small, careless crudity, and for him it turned out to be a judgment.

O how very much I wished at the time that he might become angry, might defend himself, might scream at me! He did nothing about it, all that I had to do myself, on the inside. He would have smiled if he could have. That he could not do so, with that I best saw how very much I had affected him.

And in that Pistorius suffered the blow from me, from his forward and ungrateful student, so mutely, in that he kept quiet and allowed me the right, in that he recognized my word as his fate, he made me hateful to myself, he made my thoughtlessness a thousand times greater. When I struck I had meant to hit someone strong and capable of defending himself — now there was a quiet, patiently enduring man, a defenseless one who surrendered in silence.

A long time we remained lying before the gradually dying fire, in which each glowing figure, each wriggling ashen-stick recalled the happy, beautiful, rich hours and heaped up larger and larger the guilt of my obligation to Pistorius. At last I couldn't take it anymore. I stood up and left. Long I stood before his door, long upon the dark steps, longer still outside his house waiting to see whether he would perhaps come and follow after me. Then I proceeded on and walked for hours and hours through town and suburbs, park and wood until evening. And then I sensed for the first time the mark of Cain upon my forehead.

Only gradually did I come to a state of reflection. My thoughts all had the design of accusing me and defending Pistorius. And they all ended up with the opposite of that. A thousand times I was ready to repent and take back my rash word — but yet it had been true. Only now was I able to understand Pistorius, to build up his whole dream before me. This dream had been to be a priest, to proclaim the new religion, to present new forms of exaltation, love, and adoration, to set up new symbols. But this was not his strength, not his office. He tarried all too warmly in the had-been, he knew all too exactly the former time, he was all too well-informed about Egypt, about India, about Mithras, about Abraxas. His love was tied to images which the earth had already seen, and in view of that he well knew in his innermost heart that the New had to be new and different, that it had to issue from fresh soil and not be drawn from collections and libraries. His office was perhaps to help lead men to themselves, as he had done with me. To give them the unheard of, the new gods, that was not his office.

And here the cognizance burnt me suddenly like a sharp flame: — for each person there is an "office," but for none is there one that he may himself choose, transfer, and administer as he pleases. It was false to want new gods, it was completely false to want to give the world anything whatsoever! There was no, no, no duty for an awakened man other than this one thing: to seek oneself, to become steadfast in oneself, no matter where it might lead. — That shook me deeply, and that was the fruit of this experience for me. Often I had toyed with images of the future, I had dreamed of roles that I might be destined for, perhaps as poet or as prophet, or as painter, or something akin. All that was nothing. I was not here to write poetry, to preach, to paint, neither I nor anyone else was here for that. All that took place only incidentally. Each man's true calling was only this one thing: coming to oneself. He might end up as poet or as madman, as prophet or as criminal — this was not his concern, indeed this was ultimately of no importance. His concern was to find his own destiny, not an arbitrary one, and live it out in himself, complete and unbroken. Anything else was only half, was an attempt to run away, was a flight back to the ideals of the masses, was conformity and anxiety before one's own inner self. Terrible and holy this new image arose before me, a hundred times surmised, perhaps often already expressed, and yet only now experienced. I was a cast of Nature, a cast into the uncertain, perhaps to something new, perhaps to nothing, and to let this cast take effect from the primeval depths, to feel its will within me and to make it wholly mine, that alone was my calling. That alone!

Much loneliness it had already cost me. Now I suspected that it went deeper, and that it was inescapable. I made no attempt to reconcile with Pistorius. We remained friends, but the relationship was altered. Only one single time we spoke about it, or actually it was only he who did. He said: "I have the wish to be a priest, this you know. I would most like to become the priest of the new religion, from which we have had so many presentiments. I will never be capable of it — I know it and have known it, without completely admitting it to myself, for a long time now. I will just do other priestly services, perhaps on the organ, perhaps elsewhere. But I must always be surrounded by something that I feel to be beautiful and holy, organ music and mystery, symbol and myth, I need these and will not relinquish them. — That is my weakness. For I know sometimes, Sinclair, I know at times, that I should not have such wishes, that they are a luxury and a weakness. It would be greater, it would be more correct if I were to stand quite simply at the disposal of fate, without claims. But that I cannot do; it is the one thing that I cannot do. Perhaps you will be able to do it some day. It is difficult, it is the one really difficult thing there is, my boy. I have often dreamed of it, but I cannot do it, it makes me shudder: I cannot stand so completely naked and alone, also I am a poor, weak dog that needs some warmth and food and occasionally would like to feel the nearness of his kind. He who really wants nothing at all other than his fate, he no longer has his kind, he stands completely alone and has only the cold cosmic space around him. You know, that is Jesus in the Garden of Gethsemane. There have been martyrs who gladly let themselves be nailed to the cross, but even they were no heroes, were not set free, even they wanted something to which they were dearly accustomed and which was like home, they had models, they had ideals. He who wants only his fate has neither models nor ideals anymore, he has nothing endearing, nothing consoling! And this is the way one must actually go. People like you and I are indeed quite lonely, but we still have each other at least, we have the secret satisfaction of being different, of offering resistance, of wishing for the unusual. That too must fall by the way if one wants to completely go on the way. He also dare not think of being a revolutionary, an example, a martyr. It is not to be imagined..."

No, it was not to be imagined. But it was to be dreamed, to be felt beforehand, to be surmised. A few times I had felt something of it, when

I found a completely quiet hour. Then I gazed into myself and saw the image of my fate with its open-staring eyes. They could be full of wisdom, they could be full of madness, they could radiate love or deep malice, it was all the same. Nothing therefrom was one allowed to choose, nothing was one allowed to want... One was only allowed to want oneself, one's fate. To that end Pistorius had served a long stretch as my leader.

In those days I walked around as if blind, storms raged in me, every step was danger. I saw nothing but the abysmal darkness before me, into which all hitherto existing paths ran off and downward sank. And in my inner self I saw the image of the leader, who resembled Demian and in whose eyes my fate rested.

I wrote on a piece of paper: "A leader has abandoned me. I stand completely in the dark. I cannot take a step alone. Help me!"

This I wanted to send to Demian. But I refrained; each time I wanted to do it, it looked silly and senseless. But I knew the little prayer by heart and often recited it to myself. It accompanied me every hour. I began to get an inkling of what prayer is.

My schooldays were over. I was to take a trip during vacation, my father had thought it up himself, and then I was to attend the university. As to which faculty, this I did not know. I was granted one semester of philosophy. I would have been just as content with any other.

CHAPTER SEVEN. FRAU EVA

Once during vacation I went to the house in which years before Max Demian had lived with his mother. An old woman was strolling in the garden, I addressed her and came to know that the house belonged to her. I asked after Demian's family. She remembered them well. But she didn't know where they lived now. Since she sensed my interest, she took me along into the house, brought out a leather album and showed me a photograph of Demian's mother. I could hardly remember her anymore. But as I now saw the small likeness, my heart stood still. — It was my dream image! That was she, the tall, almost manly figure of a woman, similar to her son, with traits of motherliness, traits of sternness, traits of deep passion, beautiful and alluring, beautiful and unapproachable, daemon and mother, fate and beloved. That was she!

Like a wild wonder it went through me when I came to know that my dream image existed on earth! There was a woman who looked like that, who bore the features of my fate! Where was she? Where? — And she was Demian's mother.

Soon thereafter I began my journey. A strange journey! I traveled restlessly from place to place, after every fancy, ever in quest of this woman. There were days when I hit upon nothing but forms that reminded me of her, sounded just like her, resembled her, that enticed me through the streets of unfamiliar towns, through railway stations, into trains, as in complicated dreams. There were other days when I perceived how useless my search was; then I would sit inactive somewhere in a park, in a hotel garden, in a waiting room and look inside me and try to make the image within me come alive. But it had now become shy and fleeting. Never could I sleep, only on railway journeys through unknown landscapes would I fall asleep for quarter hours. Once, in Zurich, a woman waylaid me, a pretty, somewhat fresh woman. I hardly saw her and went on as if she didn't exist. I would rather have died immediately than to have shown interest in another woman even for only an hour.

I sensed that my fate was drawing me along, I sensed that the fulfillment was near, and I was mad with impatience at not being able to do anything about it. Once at a railway station, I believe it was in Innsbruck, I saw at the window in a train that was just departing a figure that reminded me of her, and was unhappy for days. Again at night in a dream, I awoke with an ashamed and desolate feeling at the senselessness of my chase and took a direct path back home.

A few weeks later I enrolled at the University of H. Everything disappointed me. The course of lectures on the history of philosophy, which I attended, was just as insubstantial and mass-produced as the activities of the studying youngsters. Everything was so mechanical, one did like the other, and the heated gaiety on the boyish faces looked so depressingly empty and ready-made! But I was free, I had the whole day to myself, lived nice and quietly in an old ruin outside the town and had lying on the table a few volumes of Nietzsche. With him I lived, felt the loneliness of his soul, scented the fate that irresistibly drove him, suffered with him, and was blissful that there had been someone who had gone his way so inexorably.

Late in the evening once I sauntered through the town, an autumn wind blowing, and heard from the taverns the student fraternities singing. From open windows issued forth tobacco smoke in clouds, and in a thick swell of song, loud and taut, but un-exhilarating and lifelessly uniform.

I stood on a street corner and listened; out of two bars resounded the punctually executed liveliness of the youth in the night. Everywhere community, everywhere crouching together, everywhere the unloading of fate and flight into warm herd-nearness!

Behind me two men went past slowly. I heard a piece of their conversation.

"Isn't it exactly like the young men's house in a Negro village?" said the one. "Anything goes, even tattooing is yet in fashion. You see, that is the young Europe."

The voice sounded singularly admonishing — familiar. I followed the two of them down the dark lane. The one was a Japanese, small and elegant; under a street-lantern I saw his yellow smiling face begin to gleam.

Then the other one spoke again.

"Well, I expect it's no better by you in Japan either. The people who do not follow the crowd are rare everywhere. There are some here too."

Each word permeated me with a joyful terror. I recognized the speaker. It was Demian.

In the wind-swept night I followed him and the Japanese through the dark lanes, listened to their conversation and enjoyed the sound of Demian's voice. It had the old tone, it had the old, beautiful certainty and calm, and it had the power over me. Now all was well. I had found him.

At the end of a suburban street the Japanese took his leave and unlocked his front door. Demian went back the same way, I had stopped and was waiting for him in the middle of the street. With beating heart I saw him advance to meet me, upright and elastic, in a brown rubber rain-coat, a thin walking stick hanging on his arm. He came without altering his regular pace, until he was right there before me, removed his hat and showed me his old bright countenance with the resolute mouth and the peculiar brightness on the broad forehead.

"Demian!" I cried.

He reached out his hand toward me.

"So there you are, Sinclair! I've been expecting you."

"Did you know that I was here?"

"I didn't exactly know it, but I certainly hoped so. I first saw you this evening, you were following us the whole time, you know."

"So you recognized me right away?

"Naturally. You have changed to be sure. But you have the mark, yes?"

"The mark? What kind of mark?"

"We called it earlier the mark of Cain, if you can still recall. It is our mark. You have always had it, that is why I became your friend. But now, it has become more distinct."

"I didn't know that. Or actually I did. I once painted a picture of you, Demian, and was amazed that it also resembled me. Was that the mark?"

"That was it. Good, that you are here now! My mother too will be pleased."

I was startled.

"Your mother? Is she here? But she doesn't even know a thing about me."

"Oh, she knows about you. She will recognize you even without my saying who you are. — There has been nothing heard from you for a long time."

"Oh, I often wanted to write, but it didn't happen. For some time I've sensed that I would have to find you soon. I've waited for it every day."

He thrust his arm under mine and proceeded with me. We soon chatted as we had in the past. We made mention of our schooldays, of Confirmation instruction, also of that unhappy get-together that time during my vacation — only of the earliest and tightest bond between us, of the business with Kromer, was there even now no discussion.

Unexpectedly we were in the midst of an odd and ominous conversation. Suggesting a similar note to that dialogue of Demian with the Japanese, we had spoken of student life and from there had come to something else that seemed to lie far off; yet it combined in Demian's words to form an intimate connection.

He spoke of the spirit of Europe and of the sign of the times. Everywhere, he said, coalition and herd-education ruled, but nowhere freedom and love. All this communion, from the student associations and the choral unions to the states, was a forced organization, it was a communion born out of dread, out of fear, out of embarrassment, and they were rotten and old on the inside and close to collapse.

"Communion," said Demian, "is a beautiful thing. But what we see flourishing everywhere is not that at all. It will newly arise from the individuals knowing one another, and it will re-form the world for a while. Men flee to each other because they are afraid of each other — the masters for themselves, the workers for themselves, the scholars for themselves! And why are they afraid? A man is only afraid when he is not one with himself. They are afraid because they have never gotten to know themselves. A community of nothing but men who are afraid of the unknown in themselves! They all feel that the rules in their life no longer apply, that they live according to old tablets, neither their religions nor their morals, nothing of all that is in keeping with what we need. For a hundred years and more Europe has still only studied and built factories! They know exactly how many grams of powder it takes to kill a man, but they don't know how to pray to God, they don't even know how to be content for a single hour. Just look once at a student's clubhouse! Or even a pleasure resort, where the rich people go! Hopeless! — Dear Sinclair, nothing good can come of all this. These men who get together so anxiously are full of anguish and full of malice, no one trusts the other. They cling to ideals that no longer exist, and stone anyone who sets up a new ideal. I sense that there will be altercations. They will come, believe me, they will be coming soon! Naturally they will not 'improve' the world. Whether the workers kill their manufacturers, or whether Russia and Germany shoot at each other, it will only mean a change in ownership. But yet it will not have been in vain. It will demonstrate the worthlessness of present-day ideals, it will be a clearing away of Stone Age gods. This world, as it now exists, wants to die, it wants to go under, and it will."

"And what will become of us thereby?"

"Of us? Oh, perhaps we'll go under along with it. They can certainly kill our kind as well. Except that we aren't done away with by that. Around what remains of us, or around those of us who survive, the will of the future will gather. The will of mankind will show itself, which our Europe has shouted down for a time with its annual fair of technics and science. And then it will be shown that the will of mankind is never and nowhere equal with the present-day communities, the states and peoples, the associations and churches. But that which Nature wants with men stands written in the individual, it stood in Jesus, it stood in Nietzsche. For these alone important currents — which naturally can appear different every day, there will be room, when the present-day societies collapse."

It was late when we made a halt before a garden on the river.

"We live here," said Demian. "Come visit us soon! We very much expect you."

Joyfully I walked the long way home through the now grown cool night. Here and there students made a racket and staggered through town on their way home. I had often been aware of the contrast between their comical kind of merriment and my lonely life, often with a feeling of privation, often with scorn. But never before had I felt so as today with calm and secret strength, how little mattered to me, how remote and forgotten this world was for me. I remembered functionaries in my hometown, old, worthy gentlemen, who clung to the memories of their dissipated university term as to mementos of a blissful paradise and fashioned a cult with the vanished "freedom" of these student years, as otherwise some poet or other Romantic dedicates one to childhood. Everywhere the same! Everywhere they sought "freedom" and "happiness" somewhere behind themselves in the past, out of pure fear, that they might be reminded of their own responsibility and urged on their own way. A few years of boozing and jubilation, and then one crawled under and became a serious man in the civil service. Yes, it was rotten, rotten with us, and this student stupidity was less stupid and less bad than a hundred others.

When I arrived, however, at my remote dwelling and sought my bed, all these thoughts had flown away, and my entire sense hung waitingly on the great promise that this day had given to me. As soon as I wanted, tomorrow even, I could see Demian's mother. Let the students hold to their bars and to tattooing their faces, let the world be rotten and await its destruction — what did it matter to me! I was waiting for one thing, to see my destiny step toward me in a new form.

I slept soundly until late in the morning. The new day dawned for me as a solemn feast day, as I had no longer experienced since the Christmas celebrations of my boyhood. I was full of the innermost unrest, but without any fear. I felt that an important day had dawned for me, I saw and experienced the world around me here as changed, waiting, connection-full and solemn, even the softly flowing autumn rain was beautiful, tranquil, and festively full of serious-joyous music. For the first time the outer world rang clearly together with my inner one — then it is a festival of the soul, then it pays to be alive. No house, no display window, no face on the street disturbed me, all was as it had to be, but didn't carry the empty face of the commonplace and the usual, was Nature in waiting rather, respectfully ready to meet its fate. Thus had I as a little boy seen the world on the morning of the great feast days, on Christmas Day or Easter. I had not known that this world could still be so beautiful. I had gotten used to living within myself and satisfying myself therewith, that for me the sense of that out there was just lost, that the loss of the glittering colors was inevitably connected with the loss of childhood, and that in a certain measure one had to pay for the freedom and manhood of the soul with the renunciation of this lovely shimmer. Now I saw with delight that all this had only been obstructed and obscured and that it was possible, even as one who had become free and had renounced the happiness of childhood, to see the world shine and to taste the intimate thrill of childlike seeing.

The hour came when I again found the suburban garden where I had taken leave of Demian that night. Hidden behind high, rain-gray trees stood a small house, bright and habitable, tall flowering plants behind a large glass partition, behind shiny windows dark chamber walls with pictures and rows of books. The front door led directly into a small, heated hallway, a mute old maid, in black with a white apron, led me in and took my overcoat.

She left me alone in the hallway. I looked around, and immediately was in the middle of my dream. High up on the dark wood-paneled wall, above a door, there hung under glass in a black frame a well-known picture, my bird with the golden-yellow sparrow hawk's head, rising out of the world shell. Deeply moved, I remained standing there — so joyful and woeful in my heart, as though in this moment all that I had ever done and experienced returned to me as an answer and a fulfillment. Lightning-quick I saw a multitude of images in my soul run past: my native paternal house with the old stone coat of arms above the vaulted doorway, the boy Demian, who drew the coat of arms, myself as a boy, anxiously ensnared in the evil influence of my enemy Kromer, myself as a youth at the silent table in my little schoolroom painting the bird of my yearning, the soul entangled in the net of its own threads — and all, and all up to this moment sounded in me once more, was affirmed, answered, approved of in me.

With tear-stained eyes I stared at my picture and read into myself. Then I lowered my gaze: underneath the bird image in the open doorway stood a tall woman in a dark dress. It was she.

I could not say a word. Out of a face which like that of her son was time-less and ageless and full of inspired will the beautiful, venerable woman gave me a friendly smile. Her glance was fulfillment, her greeting signified homecoming. Silently I extended my hands toward her. She grasped both of them with firm, warm hands.

"You're Sinclair. I knew you right away. Welcome!"

Her voice was deep and warm, I drank it like sweet wine. And now I looked up and into her calm face, into her black, unfathomable eyes, at her fresh, ripe mouth, at her free, princely brow, which bore the mark.

"How glad I am!" I said to her and kissed her hands. "I believe I have always been on the way my whole life long — and now I have come home."

She smiled maternally.

"One never comes home," she kindly said. "But where friendly ways run together, then the whole world appears like home for an hour."

She expressed what I had felt on the way to her. Her voice and also her words were very like those of her son, and yet quite different. Everything was riper, warmer, more self-evident. But just as how Max in former times had made a boyish impression upon nobody, so his mother did not look like the mother of a grown-up son at all, so young and sweet was the tinge over her face and hair, so taut and unwrinkled was her golden skin, so radiant her mouth. More regal even than in my dream she stood before me, and her nearness was lover's bliss, her glance was fulfillment.

Thus this was the new image in which my fate showed itself to me, severe no more, isolating no more, no, ripe and full of delight! I formed no resolutions, took no vows — I had attained a goal, a high point on the way, from there on the wider way showed itself wide and magnificent, striving toward lands of promise, shaded over by treetops near to happiness, cooled by nearby gardens of every pleasure. Whatever might happen to me, I was blessed in the world to know this woman, to drink her voice and breathe her nearness. She might become mother, beloved, goddess to me — if only she was there! if only my way was near to hers!

She pointed upwards to my sparrow hawk picture.

"You never gave our Max a greater pleasure than with this picture," she said reflectively. "And me too. We were waiting for you, and when the picture came, then we knew you were on the way to us. When you were a little boy, Sinclair, my son came home from school and said: there is a youngster there who has the mark on his forehead, he must become my friend. That was you. You have not had it easy, but we have trusted in you.

One time when you were home for vacation you met up with Max again. You were sixteen years old or so at the time. Max told me about it…"

I interrupted: "Oh, he told you about that! That was my most miserable period at the time!"

"Yes, Max said to me: now Sinclair has the hardest part before him. He is making an attempt once more yet to take refuge in the community, he has even joined the bar fraternity; but he will not succeed. His mark is veiled, but it burns him secretly. — Was it not so?"

"Oh, yes, so it was, exactly so. Then I found Beatrice and then at last a leader came again to me. His name was Pistorius. Only then did it become clear to me why my period of boyhood had been so bound to Max, why I could not get loose from him. Dear lady — dear mother, I often believed at the time that I would have to take my life. Is then the way for everyone so hard?

She passed her hand over my hair, light as air.

"It is always hard, being born. You know, the bird has trouble coming out of the egg. Think back and ask yourself: was the way so hard then? Only hard? Was it not beautiful as well? Would you know of a more beautiful one, an easier one?"

I shook my head.

"It was hard," I said as if asleep, "it was hard until the dream came."

She nodded and looked at me piercingly.

"Yes, one must find his dream, then the way becomes easy. But there is no everlasting dream, each one is replaced by a newer one, and none should be held fast to."

I was deeply alarmed. Was that already a warning? Was that already a warding off? But no matter, I was ready to let her lead me and not ask after the goal.

"I do not know," I said, "how long my dream is supposed to last. I wish it could be forever. Under the picture of the bird my fate has received me, like a mother, and like a sweetheart. I belong to that fate and to no one else."

"So long as the dream is your fate, so long you should remain true to it," she earnestly confirmed.

A sadness gripped me, and the yearning wish in this enchanted hour to die. I felt the tears — how infinitely long since I had last wept! — well up irresistibly in me and overpower me. Violently I turned away from her, stepped to the window and looked with blind eyes out over the potted flowers.

Behind me I heard her voice, it sounded composed and yet was so full of tenderness like a beaker filled to the brim with wine.

"Sinclair, you are a child! Your fate does love you. One day it will belong to you completely, just as you dream it, if you remain true."

I had regained control of myself and turned my face toward her once more. She gave me her hand.

"I have a few friends," she said smiling, "a precious few, very close friends who call me Frau Eva. You too shall call me by that name if you wish."

She led me to the door, opened it and pointed into the garden. "You will find Max out there."

Under the tall trees I stood stunned and staggered, more awake or more dreaming than ever, I knew not. Gently the rain dropped from the branches. I walked slowly into the garden, which stretched far along the river bank. Finally I found Demian. He stood in an open little summer house, with a naked upper body and doing boxing exercises before a suspended punching-bag.

Astonished I came to a standstill. Demian looked splendid, the broad chest, the firm, manly head, the raised arms with tautened muscles were strong and capable, the movements came forth from hips, shoulders, and elbow joints like sporting fountains.

"Demian!" I cried. "What are you doing there?"

He laughed merrily.

"I'm practicing. I've promised the little Japanese a boxing match, the fellow is agile as a cat and naturally just as tricky. But he won't be able to deal with me. There's a very small humiliation for which I am indebted to him."

He put on his shirt and coat.

"You were already by to see my mother?"

"Yes, Demian, what a marvelous mother you have! Frau Eva! The name suits her perfectly, she is like the mother of all living things."

He looked reflectively into my face for a moment.

"You know her name already? You can be proud, young man! You are the first to whom she has already said it in the first hour."

From this day on I went in and out of the house like a son or brother, but also like a lover. When I closed the gate behind me, yes, even when from afar I saw the tall trees of the garden appear, I was rich and happy. Outside was "reality," outside was streets and houses, men and arrangements, libraries and lecture rooms — here inside, however, was love and soul, here lived the fairy tale and the dream. And yet we lived in no way cut off from the world, we often lived in the midst of it, only on a different plane, we were divided from the majority of men not through boundaries but through a different method of seeing. Our task was to represent an island in the world, perhaps a prototype, in any case, however, to be the living declaration of a different possibility. I, the long time loner, had become acquainted with the communion which is possible between men who have tasted fully being alone. Nevermore did I desire to return to the tables of the happy, to the feasts of the merry, nevermore did envy or homesickness come flying up to me when I saw the commonalities of the others. And slowly I became initiated into the secret of those who carried "the mark" on themselves.

We, those with the mark, might rightly be regarded in the world as odd, indeed as insane and dangerous. We were awakened ones, or awakening ones, and our striving expanded into an ever more complete being awake, while the striving and happiness seeking of the others was aimed at binding their opinions, their ideals and duties, their life and happiness ever more tightly to those of the herd. There, too, was striving, there, too, was strength and greatness. But whereas we, in our opinion, we marked ones represented the will of Nature to something new, set apart, and of the future, the others lived in a will of the permanent. For them mankind — which they loved as did we — was something finished, something which had to be preserved and protected. For us mankind was a distant future, towards which we were all on the way, whose form no one knew, whose laws stood written down nowhere.

Outside of Frau Eva, Max, and myself there belonged to our circle, nearer or farther, yet many a seeker of a very diverse sort. Many of them walked a particular path, had set distinct goals for themselves and clung to particular opinions and duties, amongst them were astrologers and cabalists, also an adherent of Count Tolstoy, and also all kinds of tender, shy, vulnerable men, adherents of new sects, fosterers of Indian disciplines, vegetarians and others. With all these we actually had nothing spiritual in common except the respect which each did not begrudge to the secret dream-life of the other. Others stood nearer to us who pursued the search of mankind for gods and new ideals in the past, and whose studies often reminded me of my Pistorius. They brought books with them, translated texts to us of ancient languages, showed us illustrations of ancient symbols and rites and taught us to see how mankind's entire possession of ideals hitherto consisted of dreams of the unconscious soul, of dreams in which mankind gropingly followed the inklings of its future possibilities. Thus we ran through the wonderful, thousand-headed tangle of gods of the ancient world up to the hither-dawning of the Christian conversion. The confessions of the lonesome pious ones we became acquainted with, and the changes of religions from nation to nation. And from all that we gathered was yielded to us a critique of our time and of present-day Europe, that with enormous efforts had created mankind's powerful new weapons but which finally proved to be in the end a deep and flagrant desolation of the spirit. For it had gained the whole world, only to lose its soul.

Here also there were believers and confessors of decided hopes and doctrines of salvation. There were Buddhists who wanted to convert Europe, and Tolstoy disciples, and other creeds. We in the immediate circle heard and accepted none of these teachings as other than allegories. We marked ones had no worry over the shape of the future. To us every creed, every doctrine of salvation already seemed dead and useless beforehand. And we felt only this as a duty and destiny: that each one of us would so completely become himself, so completely become suitable to the working germ of Nature within him and to live as he pleased, so that the uncertain future would find us ready for each and every thing that she might bring.

Then this was, said or unsaid, a distinct feeling in us all, that a new birth and a collapse of the present was nigh and already perceptible. Demian said to me at times: "What will come is unimaginable. The soul of Europe is an animal that has lain fettered endlessly long. When it becomes free, its first movements will not be the loveliest. But the ways and by-ways are of no consequence, if only the true need of the soul comes to light, which has been lied away and benumbed again and again for so long. Then our day will come, then they will need us, not as leaders or new lawgivers — the new laws we will no longer live to see —, rather as willing ones, as such who are ready to come along and to stand there, at the place whither fate calls them. Look, all men are ready to do the incredible when their ideals are threatened. But no one is there when a new ideal, a new, perhaps dangerous and uncanny stirring of growth knocks. The few, who are there then and come along, we will be. We are marked for that purpose — as Cain was marked, to arouse fear and hatred and to drive the humanity of that time out of a narrow idyll into dangerous expanses. All men who have had an effect on the progress of mankind, all of them without exception, were only therefor capable and effective because they were fate-ready. That goes for Moses and Buddha, it goes for Napoleon and Bismarck. Which wave one serves, from which pole he is ruled, that is not his choice. If Bismarck had understood the Social Democrats and put himself in their ranks, then he would have been a clever master but not a man of destiny. So it was with Napoleon, with Caesar, with Loyola, with all of them! One must always think in terms of biology and historical development! When the upheavals on the earth's surface threw the sea creatures onto the land, the land creatures into the sea, it was fate-ready specimens that accomplished the new and unheard-of and could save their kind through new adaptations. Whether it was these same specimens which previously stood out in their species as conservative and preserving ones, or rather the eccentrics and revolutionaries, that we do not know. They were ready and therefore could deliver their species across into new developments. That we know. That is why we want to be ready."

During such conversations Frau Eva was often present, yet she herself did not participate in this manner. She was for each of us who expressed his thoughts a listener and an echo, full of trust, full of understanding; it seemed as if all the thoughts came from her and returned to her. To sit near her, to hear her voice now and then and to take part in the atmosphere of ripeness and soul, which surrounded her, was happiness for me.

She perceived it at once, if there was any change in me, a dampening or a renewing in my gait. It seemed to me as if the dreams I had in sleep were suggestions from her. I often recounted them to her, and they were under-standable and natural to her, there were no peculiarities in them that she could not follow with a clear feeling. For a time I had dreams which were like copies of our daily conversations. I dreamed that the entire world was in an uproar and that I, alone or with Demian, tensely awaited the great fate. The fate remained veiled, but somehow bore the features of Frau Eva — to be chosen or to be rejected by her, that was the fate.

Sometimes she said with a smile: "Your dream is not complete, Sinclair, you have forgotten the best part —" and it could happen that then it would occur to me again and I could not comprehend how I could have forgotten it.

At times I became discontented and tortured with desire. I thought I could no longer stand seeing her next to me without embracing her. This too she noticed right away. Once when I stayed away for several days and came back troubled, she took me aside and said: "You should not give yourself up to wishes which you do not believe in. I know what you are wishing for. You must be able to give up these wishes or wish for them completely and correctly. Once you are capable of asking in such a way that you are quite certain of the fulfillment in itself, then the fulfillment is there as well. You wish, however, and regret it again, and have anxiety thereby. I want to tell you a fable."

And she told me of a young man who had fallen in love with a star. By the sea he stood, reached his hands out, and prayed to the star; he dreamed of it and fixed all his thoughts on it. But he knew, or thought he knew, that a star cannot be embraced by a man. He regarded it as his fate to love a heavenly body without hope of fulfillment, and he built out of these thoughts an entire life story of renunciation and mute, faithful suffering that was to improve and purify him. All his dreams, however, were wholly given up to the star. One time he stood again at night by the sea upon a high cliff and gazed at the star and burned with love for it. And in a moment of the greatest yearning he made the leap and threw himself into the void, towards the star. But in the moment of the leaping he yet thought lightning-fast: it is still impossible after all! He lay there below on the strand and was shattered. He did not understand how to love. Had he had the strength of soul, in the moment when he leaped, to believe firmly and surely in the fulfillment, he would have flown upwards and been united with the star.

"Love must not entreat," she said, "nor demand either. Love must have the strength to come to certainty in itself. Then it is no longer attracted, but attracts. Sinclair, your love is attracted to me. If it attracts me for once, then I will come. I want to present no gifts, I want to be won."

Another time, however, she told me a different fable. There was a lover who loved without hope. He withdrew entirely into his soul and thought himself burnt to death from love. He was lost to the world, he saw the blue sky and the green wood no more, the brook did not rush for him, the harp did not sound for him, everything was sunk, and he had become poor and miserable. His love grew, however, and he would much rather have died or come to ruin than renounce possession of the beautiful woman that he loved. Then he sensed how his love had burnt up everything else in him, and it became mighty and drew and drew, and the beautiful woman was obliged to follow, she came, he stood with outstretched arms, to draw her to himself. As she stood before him, however, she was completely transformed, and he looked and felt with a shudder that he had drawn the entire lost world hither to himself. She stood before him and surren-dered herself to him, sky and wood and brook, all in new colors fresh and glorious came to meet him, belonged to him, spoke his language. And instead of merely winning a woman, he had the whole world close to his heart, and every star in the sky glowed in him and sparkled joy through his soul. — He had loved and thereby found himself. But most people love in order to thereby lose themselves.

My love for Frau Eva seemed to me to be the sole contents of my life. But every day it had a different look. Sometimes I thought I felt for certain that it was not her person toward which my being strove to be attracted, but that she was only a symbol of my inner self and would only lead me deeper within myself. Often I heard words from her which sounded to me like answers of my unconscious to burning questions that moved me. Then again there were moments in which I burned with sensual desire next to her and kissed objects which she had touched. And little by little, sensual and un-sensual love, reality and symbol slid themselves one upon the other. Then it would happen that while at home in my room I would think on her, in peaceful intimacy, and thereby believed I felt her hand in mine and her lips on mine. Or I was beside her, looked her in the face, spoke with her and heard her voice and yet did not know whether she was real and not a dream. I began to get an inkling of how one can possess a lasting and undying love. I would have by the reading of a book a new insight, and it was the same feeling as a kiss from Frau Eva. She stroked my hair and smiled her ripe, fragrant warmth toward me, and I had the same feeling as when I made an advance into myself. All that was important and was fate for me, her figure could take on. She could transform herself into each of my thoughts and each could transform itself into her.

On the Christmas holidays, during which I was with my parents, I was afraid because I thought it would be torture to live for two weeks away from Frau Eva. But it was no torture, it was glorious, to be at home and to think of her. When I came back to H. I still stayed away from her house for two days, in order to enjoy this security and independence from her physical presence. I also had dreams in which my union with her was effected in new allegorical modes. She was a sea into which I streamingly flowed. She was a star, and I myself was on the way to her as a star, and we met each other and felt ourselves drawn to each other, remained together and revolved blissfully for all time in close, resounding circles round each other.

This dream I related to her when I first visited her again.

"The dream is beautiful," she said quietly. "Make it come true!"

In early springtime came a day which I have never forgotten. I walked into the hallway, a window stood open, and a lukewarm air current rolled the heavy aroma of hyacinths through the room. Since nobody was to be seen there, I went up the steps into Max Demian's study. I knocked lightly on the door and entered without waiting for a summons, as was my custom.

The room was dark, all the curtains were drawn. The door to a small adjoining room stood open, where Max had set up a chemical laboratory. From there came the bright, white light of the spring sun, which shone through rainclouds. I thought there was nobody there and drew back one of the curtains.

Then I saw Max Demian sitting on a footstool near the curtained window, huddled all together and strangely altered, and like a flash the feeling ran through me: you have experienced this once before! His arms hung motionless, his hand in his lap, his somewhat forward-inclined face with open eyes was look-free and dead, in one pupil a small, glaring light reflex had a lifeless gleam, as in a piece of glass. His pale countenance was sunk in itself and without expression other than a tremendous stiffness, it looked like a primeval animal mask at the portal of a temple. He seemed not to be breathing.

Memory made me shudder all over — thus, exactly thus had I seen him once before, many years ago, when I was still a little boy. Thus had the eyes stared inwardly, thus had the hands been laid lifelessly next to each other, a fly had wandered across his face. And he had at that time, perhaps six years ago, looked exactly as old and as timeless, not a wrinkle in his face was different today.

Overcome by fear I went quietly out of the room and down the stairs. In the hallway I met Frau Eva. She was pale and seemed tired, which I had never known her to be, a shadow traveled across the window, the glaring, white sun had suddenly disappeared.

"I was with Max," I whispered quickly. "Has something happened? He's either asleep or lost in thought, I don't know, I saw him once before like that some time ago."

"You didn't wake him, did you?" she asked quickly.

"No. He didn't hear me. I went right out again. Frau Eva, tell me, what is it with him?"

She passed the back of her hand across her forehead.

"Don't worry, Sinclair, nothing will happen to him. He has withdrawn into himself. It won't last long."

She stood up and went out into the garden, although it had just begun to rain. I sensed that I should not come along. So I walked up and down the hallway, inhaled the narcotic-scented hyacinths, stared at my bird picture above the doorway, and breathed with oppression the strange shadow which had filled the house that morning. What was that? What had happened?

Frau Eva came back directly. Drops of rain clung to her dark hair. She sat down in her armchair. Weariness lay over her. I walked up next to her, bent over her, and kissed the drops out of her hair. Her eyes were bright and calm, but the drops tasted like tears to me.

"Should I look after him?" I asked in a whisper.

She smiled weakly.

"Don't be a little boy, Sinclair!" she admonished me loudly, as if in order to break a spell within herself. "Go now and come again later, I cannot talk with you now."

I walked and ran away from the house and the town toward the mountains, the slanting thin rain came to meet me in the face, the clouds drifted along low under heavy pressure as though in anguish. Below there was hardly any wind, up above it appeared to storm, more than once the sun, pale and glaring, momentarily broke through the steel cloud of gray.

Then drifting across the heavens came a loose yellow cloud, it jammed itself up against the gray wall, and in a few seconds the wind formed out of the yellow and blue an image, an immense bird, which tore itself loose from the blue hurly-burly and with broad beating of wings vanished into the heavens. Then the storm became audible, and rain mixed with hail rattled down. A brief, improbable, and terrible sounding thunder crackled over the scourged landscape, immediately thereupon a glimpse of sun broke through once more, and upon the nearby mountains above the brown woods shone fallow and unreal the pale snow.

When I returned wet and wind-blown after some hours, Demian himself opened the front door for me.

He took me with him up to his room, in the laboratory a gas flame was burning, papers lay all around, he seemed to have been working.

"Take a seat," he invited me, "you must be tired, it was horrible weather, one can see that you were outside all right. Tea is coming just now."

"Something is wrong today," I began hesitantly, "it can't only be that little bit of thunderstorm."

He looked at me searchingly.

"Have you seen something?"

"Yes. I distinctly saw for a moment in the clouds an image."

"What kind of image?"

"It was a bird."

"The sparrow hawk? Was that it? Your dreambird?"

"Yes, it was my sparrow hawk. It was yellow and gigantic and flew off into the blue-black sky."

Demian took a deep breath.

There was a knock at the door. The old maidservant brought the tea.

"Take some, Sinclair, please. — I believe you didn't see the bird by chance?"

"By chance? Does one see such things by chance?"

"Well, no. It signifies something. Do you know what?"

"No. I only sense that it signifies a convulsion, a stride in fate. I believe it concerns us all."

He walked back and forth furiously.

"A stride in fate!" he cried loudly. "I dreamt the same thing last night, and yesterday my mother had a presentiment that said the like. — I dreamt I was climbing up a ladder placed against a tree trunk or tower. When I was at the top I could see the whole countryside, it was a large plain, with towns and villages burning. I cannot yet recount it all, it is not yet all clear to me."

"Do you think the dream refers to you?" I asked.

"To me? Naturally. Nobody dreams what doesn't concern him. But it doesn't concern me alone, there you are right. I distinguish pretty precisely between dreams that point out to me movements within my own soul, and the others, very rare, in which the whole fate of man suggests itself. I have seldom had such dreams, and never one of which I could say it was a prophecy and proceeded to be fulfilled. The interpretations are too uncertain. But this I know for sure, I have dreamt something which does not concern me alone. The dream appertains namely to other, earlier ones which I have had and which it carries on. It is these dreams, Sinclair, from which I have the forebodings, of which I have already spoken to you. That our world is quite rotten we know, but that would still be no reason to prophesy its going-under or the like. But for several years I have had dreams, from which I conclude, or feel, or what you will — from which I thus feel, that the collapse of an old world is getting closer. They were at first very weak, distant inklings, but they have become ever clearer and stronger. Still I know nothing other than that something great and terrible is brewing that has to do with me as well. Sinclair, we will live to see this, of which we have often spoken! The world wants to renew itself. It smells of death. Nothing new can come without death. — It is more horrible than I had thought."

I stared at him horrified.

"Can't you tell me the rest of your dream?" I asked shyly.

He shook his head.

"No."

The door opened and Frau Eva came in.

"There you sit next to each other! Children, you're not sad, are you?"

She looked fresh and no longer weary at all. Demian smiled at her, she came to us like a mother does to frightened children.

"We aren't sad, mother, we've only been puzzling a little over these new signs. But it doesn't matter anyway. That which wants to come will be here suddenly, and then we will certainly find out that which we need to know."

I was in low spirits, however, and when I took my leave and walked alone through the hallway, I perceived the hyacinth scent to be faded, flat, and cadaverous. A shadow had fallen over us.

CHAPTER EIGHT. BEGINNING OF THE END

I had succeeded in being able to remain in H. for the summer semester yet. Instead of in the house, we now were almost always in the garden by the river. The Japanese, who by the way had rightly lost in the boxing match, was gone, the Tolstoyan was also absent. Demian kept a horse and rode for days and days with perseverance. I was often alone with his mother.

At times I marveled at the peacefulness of my life. I had been so long accustomed to being alone, to practicing renunciation, to struggling laboriously with my torments, that these months in H. seemed to me like a dream island, upon which I was allowed to live in comfort and enchantment among only beautiful, agreeable things and feelings. I had an inkling that this was a foretaste of that new, higher community about which we had been thinking. And always a deep sadness took hold of me over this happiness, for I well knew it could not last. I was not allotted to breathe in fullness and comfort, I needed torment and hot pursuit. I sensed: one day I would awake from these beautiful images of love and stand alone again, completely alone, in the cold world of the others, where for me there was only solitude or struggle, no peace, no living together.

Then I would nestle with double tenderness close to Frau Eva, glad that my fate still bore these fair, calm features.

The summer weeks slipped away quickly and easily, the semester was already at an end. My departure would soon be at hand, I dared not think about it, and didn't do so either, but clung to the beautiful days as a butterfly does to the honey-flower. This had been now my time of happiness, the first fulfillment of my life and my acceptance into the alliance — what would come after that? I would fight my way through once more, suffer longing, be alone.

On one of these days this presentiment took possession of me so strongly that my love for Frau Eva suddenly flamed up painfully. My God, how soon, then I would see her no more, hear no more her solid, good stride through the house, find no more her flowers upon my table! And what had I achieved? I had dreamed and lulled myself in comfort, instead of winning her, instead of struggling for her and dragging her to me forever! All that she had ever said to me about true love occurred to me, a hundred fine, warning words, a hundred soft enticements, promises perhaps — what had I made out of them? Nothing! Nothing!

I placed myself in the middle of my room, collected my entire consciousness, and thought about Eva. I wanted to summon all the powers of my soul, in order to let her feel my love, in order to draw her hither to me. She had to come and long for my embrace, my kiss had to root insatiably in her ripe love-lips.

I stood and strained myself until from my fingers and feet hither I became cold. I could feel the strength emanate from me. For a few moments something drew together firm and tight in me, something bright and cool; I had for a moment the feeling I carried a crystal in my heart, and I knew it was my ego. The coldness ascended to my breast.

When I awoke from this terrible straining I felt that something would come. I was utterly spent, but I was ready to see Eva step into the room, ardent and enraptured.

The clatter of hooves hammered now up along the long street, sounded near and harsh, then halted suddenly. I sprang to the window. Below, Demian dismounted from the horse. I ran down.

"What's wrong, Demian? Nothing's happened to your mother, has it?"

He paid no heed to my words. He was very pale, and sweat ran from both sides of his brow over his cheeks. He tied the bridle of his heated horse to the garden fence, took my arm, and went with me down the street.

"Have you heard anything yet?"

I knew nothing.

Demian pressed my arm and turned his face toward me, with a dark, sympathetic, singular look.

"Yes, my boy, now it begins. You do know of the great tension with Russia —"

"What? Is there war? I have never thought about it."

He spoke softly, although no one was nearby.

"It's not yet declared. But there will be war. You can depend on that. I didn't want to bother you anymore with the affair hitherto, but since then three times I have seen new omens. So there will be no world destruction, no earthquake, no revolution. It will be war. You will see how that catches on! It will be a delight to people, even now everyone is overjoyed at the attack-launching. So stale has their life become. — But you will see, Sinclair, this is only the beginning. Perhaps it will be a large war, a very large war. But that too is merely the beginning. The new begins, and the new, for those who cling to the old, will be terrifying. What will you do?"

I was confounded, to me it all still sounded strange and improbable.

"I don't know — and you?"

He shrugged his shoulders.

"As soon as there's mobilization, I'll report for duty. I'm a lieutenant."

"You? I didn't know a word about it."

"Yes, it was one of my adaptations. You know, I was never fond of attracting outward attention and have always rather done a little too much in order to be correct. In eight days, I believe, I'll already be in the field —"

"For God's sake —"

"Now, boy, you mustn't take this sentimentally. After all it doesn't really give me pleasure to order gunfire upon living men, but that will be incidental. Now each one of us will come in the great wheel. You too. You will surely be conscripted.

"And your mother, Demian?"

Only now I reflected again upon that which had happened a quarter hour earlier. How the world had changed! All my strength I had raked together in order to conjure the sweetest image, and now fate looked at me suddenly anew out of a menacing and gruesome mask.

"My mother? Ah, we need not worry about her. She is secure, more secure than anyone else in the world is today. — You love her that much?"

"You knew it, Demian?" He laughed heartily and quite relieved.

"Little boy! Of course I knew it! No one yet has said Frau Eva to my mother without loving her. By the way, how was that? You called either me or her today, isn't that so?"

"Yes, I called. — — I called for her.

"She sensed it. She sent me away all of a sudden, saying I must go to you. I had just told her the news about Russia."

We turned around and spoke a little more, he untied his horse and mounted up.

In my room upstairs I first sensed how exhausted I was, from Demian's message and much more still from the previous strain. But Frau Eva had heard me! I had reached her heart with my thoughts. She would have come herself — unless — — How peculiar this all was, and how fundamentally beautiful! Now there was a war coming. Now that was beginning to happen which we had talked about over and over. And Demian had known so much about it beforehand. How strange that now the stream of the world should not be running past us anymore —, that suddenly now it went through our hearts, that adventure and wild destiny called us, and that now or shortly the movement would be here when the world needed us, when it would be transformed. Demian was right, it was not to be taken sentimentally. It was only remarkable that I now should experience this so lonely matter of "fate" in common and along with so many, with the whole world. Good then!

I was ready. In the evening when I walked through the town, every corner was buzzing from the great excitement. Everywhere the word was "war"!

I came to Frau Eva's house, we ate supper in the little summerhouse. I was the only guest. No one said a word about war. Only late, shortly before I was to leave, Frau Eva said: "Dear Sinclair, you called for me today. You know why I didn't come myself. But don't forget: you now know the call, and whenever you need someone who carries the mark, then call again!" She rose and went ahead through the garden-gloaming. Tall and regal strode the mysterious one between the silent trees, and above her head glimmered small and tender the many stars.

I am coming to the end. Things went their speedy way. Soon there was war, and Demian, strangely foreign in his uniform with the silver-gray coat, went off. I brought his mother back home. Soon I too took my leave of her, she kissed me on the mouth and held me a moment on her breast, and her great eyes burned close and steadfast into mine.

And all men were as if made brothers. They thought of fatherland and honor. But it was fate, whose unveiled face they all beheld for a moment. Young men came out of barracks, climbed aboard trains, and upon many faces I saw a sign — not ours — a sign both beautiful and dignified, that meant love and death. Even I was embraced by men whom I had never seen, and I understood it and gladly gave back in return. It was an intoxication in which they did it, no fateful will, but the intoxication was sacred, it followed as a consequence of their all having had a brief, rousing look into the eyes of fate.

It was already almost winter when I entered the field of action.

In the beginning I was disappointed with everything, despite the sensations of being in a shooting spree. Earlier I had pondered much on why so extremely seldom a man was capable of living for an ideal. Now I saw that many, indeed all men, are capable of dying for an ideal. Only it could not be a personal, free chosen ideal, it had to be one that was taken on and held in common.

In time, however, I saw that I had underestimated the men. As much as the service and the common danger rendered them uniform, I still saw many, living and dying, approach that fateful will splendidly. Many, very many, not only during the attack but at any time, had the steadfast, distant, a little bit possessed look that knew nothing of goals and meant a full devotedness to the enormous. They might believe and suppose whatever they wanted — they were ready, they were useful, out of them the future would let itself be formed. And the more rigidly the world seemed focused on war and heroism, on honor and other old ideals, the more remote and improbable each voice of apparent humanity sounded, this was all only surface, just as how the question regarding the external and political goals of the war remained only surface. In the depths something was coming into existence. Something like a new humanity. For many could I see, and many of them died at my side — to them the insight had become tangible, that hatred and rage, killing and destruction were not connected with these objects. No, the objects, just like the goals, were quite accidental. The original feelings, even the wildest, were not aimed at the foe, their bloody work was only a radiance of the inner self, of the soul split-up in itself, which wanted to rage and kill, destroy and die, in order to be born anew. A gigantic bird was fighting its way out of the egg, and the egg was the world, and the world had to go to rack and ruin.

Before the farmstead that we had occupied I stood on watch one early spring night. In peevish shoves a slovenly wind went along, across the high Flemish sky rode cloud-armies, somewhere behind them the notion of a moon. Already the whole day I had been ill at ease, a worry of some sort disturbed me. Now, at my dark post, I thought warmly about the images of my former life, about Frau Eva, about Demian. I stood leaning on a poplar tree and stared into the agitated sky, whose mysteriously quivering patches of brightness soon turned into a large, flowing series of images. By the strange weakness of my pulse, by the insensibility of my skin toward wind and rain, by my sparkling inner alertness, I could sense that a leader was around me.

In the clouds there was a great city to be seen, out of which millions of people streamed forth, they spread themselves in swarms over wide landscapes. Amidst them strode a powerful divine form, sparkling stars in her hair, large as a mountain, with the features of Frau Eva. Into her disappeared the herds of people, as into a gigantic cavern, and they were gone. The goddess crouched down on the ground, bright glistened the mark on her forehead. A dream seemed to have power over her, she closed her eyes, and her vast countenance was twisted in woe. Suddenly she cried out loudly, and out of her forehead sprang stars, many thousands of shining stars, which soared in splendid arcs and semi-circles across the black sky.

One of the stars blistered toward me with a loud sound, it seemed to seek me. — Then, roaring, it cracked apart into a thousand sparks, it dragged me upward and threw me to the ground again, thunderously the world broke in pieces above me.

They found me next to the poplar tree, covered with earth and with many wounds.

I lay in a cellar, heavy guns grumbled above me. I lay in a wagon and jolted across empty fields. Mostly I slept or was without consciousness.

But the more deeply I slept, the more keenly I felt that something was drawing me, that I was following a force that was master over me.

I lay in a stable upon straw, it was dark, somebody had stepped on my hand. But my inner self wanted to go on, more strongly it drew me away. Again I lay on a wagon and later on a litter or a ladder, even more strongly I felt myself ordered to some place or another, felt nothing other than the urge to get there at last.

Then I reached my goal. It was night, I was fully conscious, just now even I had powerfully perceived the pull and urge in me. Now I lay in a hall, bedded down on the floor, and felt that I was there whither I had been called. I glanced around me, close beside my mattress lay another, and someone, upon it, who bent forward and looked at me. He had the mark on his forehead. It was Max Demian.

I could not speak, and he also could not or would not. He only looked at me. Upon his face lay the light from a lamp which hung above him on the wall. He smiled at me.

An endlessly long time he went on looking me in the eyes. Slowly he moved his face closer to mine, until we almost touched.

"Sinclair!" he said in a whisper.

I gave him a sign with my eyes to let him know I understood him.

He smiled again, almost as in pity.

"Little boy!" he said, smiling.

His mouth now lay very close to mine. Softly he continued to speak.

"Can you still remember Franz Kromer?" he asked.

I winked to him and could even smile.

"Little Sinclair, be careful! I will have to go away. Perhaps you will need me again sometime, against Kromer or otherwise. If you call me then, then I will no longer come so crudely, riding upon a horse or by rail. You must then listen within yourself, then you will note that I am within you. Do you understand? — And something else! Frau Eva said if you are ever in a bad way, then I am to give you the kiss from her that she imparted to me... Close your eyes, Sinclair!"

I obediently closed my eyes, I sensed a light kiss upon my lips, upon which I always had a little blood remaining that would never become less. And then I fell asleep.

In the morning I was awakened, I was supposed to have my wounds dressed. When I was properly awake at last, I quickly turned toward the neighboring mattress. On it there lay an unfamiliar man, whom I had never seen before.

The wound-dressing hurt. Everything that has happened to me since has hurt. But sometimes when I find the key and climb down completely into myself, there where in the dark mirror the images of fate slumber, then I need only bend over the black mirror and see my own image, that now completely resembles him, him, my friend and leader.

Printed in the United States
by Baker & Taylor Publisher Services